FEAR

AMONG THE MANY CLASSIC WORKS
By L. Ron Hubbard

Battlefield Earth
Beyond the Black Nebula
Buckskin Brigades
The Conquest of Space
The Dangerous Dimension
Death's Deputy
The Emperor of the Universe
Fear
Final Blackout
Forbidden Voyage
The Incredible Destination
The Kilkenny Cats
The Kingslayer
The Last Admiral
The Magnificent Failure
The Masters of Sleep
The Mission Earth Dekalogy★
Volume   1:   The Invader's Plan
Volume   2:   Black Genesis
Volume   3:   The Enemy Within
Volume   4:   An Alien Affair
Volume   5:   Fortune of Fear
Volume   6:   Death Quest
Volume   7:   Voyage of Vengeance
Volume   8:   Disaster
Volume   9:   Villainy Victorious
Volume 10:   The Doomed Planet
The Mutineers
Ole Doc Methuselah
Ole Mother Methuselah
The Rebels
Return to Tomorrow
Slaves of Sleep
To the Stars
The Traitor
Triton
Typewriter in the Sky
The Ultimate Adventure
The Unwilling Hero

★Dekalogy—a group of ten volumes

FEAR

L.RON HUBBARD

Bridge Publications, Inc.

10 9 8 7 6 5 4 3 2 1

Library of Congress Cataloging in Publication Data

Hubbard, L. Ron (Lafayette Ron), 1911 - 1986
　　　Fear
　　　1. Fiction, American. I. Title
　　　ISBN 0-88404-599-4 (alk. paper)

AUTHOR'S NOTE

There is one thing which I wish the reader could keep in mind throughout, and that is: this story is wholly logical, for all that will appear to the contrary. It is not a very nice story, nor should it be read alone at midnight— for it is true that any man might have the following happen to him. Even you, today, might lose four hours from your life and follow, then, in the course of James Lowry.

— *L. Ron Hubbard*

LIST OF ILLUSTRATIONS

Chapter 1..page 1
For the briefest flicker he half recalled the birth of his own wanderlust. A theft in his dorm, accusation, expulsion and disgrace...

Chapter 2..page 27
And a white shape was moving slowly toward him on soundless feet and a white face gleamed dully above a glittering knife. Nearer and nearer—

Chapter 3..page 45
"Well now, James Lowry, that's a very silly thing to do, to do, to do. To lose your hat. You are old enough to know better, and your head is big enough to keep a hat on. But that isn't all you've lost, James Lowry."

Chapter 4..page 73
It was nothing very positive, just an impression of something dark and round traveling along beside him. He jerked his head to stare at it— but there was nothing there.

Chapter 5..page 101
There was a gentle, purring sound, and the dark object loomed higher. Something began slowly to pry Lowry's fingers off the ledge.

Chapter 6..page 125
...obviously he had lost a great deal of weight, for his cheeks were sunken, and a pallor as gray as the belly of a rain cloud gave him a shock, so much did it cause him to resemble a dead man.

Chapter 7..page 145
He kicked it and it thumped slowly into the corner where its sightless sockets regarded him in mild reproach; one of its teeth had fallen out and made a brown dot on the carpet.

Chapter 8..page 171
Each face into which he looked in turn became Tommy's! And each face possessed that mocking smile and slyly evil glint of eye.

FOREWORD

Once in a while an editor sees a story that is so finely crafted that it provides immeasurable pleasure to bring it before the reader. *Fear* is just such a work, and more, for it not only has great reader appeal, it uniformly inspires awe in top authors themselves. From Ray Bradbury to Isaac Asimov, it has earned rare praise as an unforgettable, timeless classic.

Written more than fifty years ago, the story has not only withstood the test of time, but additionally, it is credited by literary historians, such as David Hartwell, for transforming and creating "the foundations of the contemporary horror genre."

Legend, too, has a habit of springing up around great works. Robert Heinlein, a close friend of L. Ron Hubbard, was fond of relating the story of how *Fear* was written on a single train ride from New York to Seattle.

But it is the impact on the reader that is the singular, most important test of any work. *Fear* delivers.

Stephen King, without question today's master of the horror genre, says it best when he looks back at the accomplishment represented by *Fear:*

> L. Ron Hubbard's *Fear* is one of the few books in the chiller genre which actually merits employment of the overworked adjective "classic," as in "This is a classic tale of creeping, surreal menace and horror." If you're not averse to a case of the cold chills—a rather bad one—and you've never read *Fear,* I urge you to do so. Don't even wait for a dark and stormy night. This is one of the really, really good ones.

In that, he is not alone. Whether read today or reread fifty years from today, the chilling impact will never fade.

Why is this?

L. Ron Hubbard did something no other author had ever successfully done. Without the use of supernatural contrivance—werewolves, vampires; without resorting to extreme venues—the haunted house-on-the-hill, the cellar lab, the strange planet; and without using super-psychotic protagonists—Freddy Kruger, Norman Bates; he took an ordinary man, in a very ordinary circumstance and descended him into a completely plausible but extraordinary *hell.*

Why is *Fear* so powerful? Because it really *could* happen. And *that* is terrifying.

That simple premise has garnered more accolades than a thousand books of wolves howling to a pale moon on a "dark and stormy night."

So, if you're not afraid of the *ordinary*, this story is for you.

But, don't say we didn't warn you...

THE EDITORS

FEAR

CHAPTER

1

For the briefest flicker he half recalled the birth of his own wanderlust. A theft in his dorm, accusation, expulsion and disgrace . . .

Lurking, that lovely spring day, in the office of Dr. Chalmers, Atworthy College Medical Clinic, there might have been two small spirits of the air, pressed back into the dark shadow behind the door, avoiding as far as possible the warm sunlight which fell gently upon the rug.

Professor Lowry, buttoning his shirt, said, "So I am good for another year, am I?"

"For another thirty-eight years," smiled Dr. Chalmers. "A fellow with a rugged build like yours doesn't have to worry much about a thing like malaria. Not even the best variety of bug Yucatan could offer. You'll have a few chills, of course, but nothing to worry about. By the way, when are you going back to Mexico?"

"If I go when my wife gives me leave, that'll be never."

"And if I had a woman as lovely as your wife Mary," said Chalmers, "Yucatan could go give its malaria to somebody else. Oh, well"—and he tried to make himself believe he was not, after all, envious of Atworthy's wandering ethnologist— "I never could see what you fellows saw in strange lands and places."

"Facts," said Lowry.

"Yes, I suppose. Facts about primitive sacrifice and demons and devils— Say, by the way, that was a very nice article you had in the *Newspaper Weekly* last Sunday."

The door moved slightly, though it might have been caused by the cool breath of verdure which came in the window.

"Thank you," said Lowry, trying not to look too pleased.

"Of course," said young Chalmers, "you were rather sticking out your neck. You had your friend Tommy frothing about such insolence. He's very fond of his demons and devils, you know."

"He likes to pose," said Lowry. "But how do you mean, 'sticking out my neck'?"

"You haven't been here much under Jebson," said Chalmers. "He nearly crucified a young mathematician for using Atworthy's name in a scientific magazine. But then, maybe our beloved president didn't see it. Can't imagine the old stuffed shirt reading the *Newspaper Weekly*, anyway."

"Oh," said Lowry. "I thought you meant about my denying the existence of such things. Tommy—"

"Well, maybe I meant that, too," said Chalmers. "I guess we're all superstitious savages at heart. And when you come out in bold-face type and ridicule ancient belief that demons caused sickness and woe and when you throw dirt, so to speak, in the faces of luck and fate, you must be very, very sure of yourself."

"Why shouldn't I be sure of myself?" said Lowry, smiling. "Did anyone ever meet a spirit of any sort face to face? I mean, of course, that there aren't any authenticated cases on record anywhere."

"Not even," said Chalmers, "the visions of saints?"

"Anyone who starves himself long enough can see visions."

"Still," said Chalmers, "when you offer so wildly to present your head in a basket to the man who can show you a sure-enough demon—"

"And my head in a basket he shall have," said Lowry. "For a man of science, you talk very weirdly, old fellow."

"I have been in a psychiatric ward often enough," said Chalmers. "At first I used to think it was the patient and then, after a while, I began to wonder. You know, demons are supposed to come out with the full moon. Ever watch a whole psychopathic ward go stark raving mad during the three days that a moon is full?"

"Nonsense."

"Perhaps."

"Chalmers, I tried, in that article, to show how people began to believe in supernatural agencies and how scientific explanation has at last superseded vague terror. Now don't come along and tell me that you can cast some doubt on those findings."

"Oh"—and Chalmers began to laugh—"we both know that 'truth' is an abstract quantity that probably doesn't exist. Go crusading against your devils and your demons, Professor Lowry. And if they get mad at you, argue them out of existence. I myself don't say they exist. It merely strikes me strangely that man's lot could be so consistently unhappy without something somewhere aiding in that misery. And if it is because electrons vibrate at certain speeds, or if it is because the spirits of air and earth and water are jealous of any comfort and happiness that man might have, I neither know nor care. But how comforting it is to knock on wood when one has made a brag."

"And so," said Lowry, slipping into his topcoat, "the goblins are gonna get me if I don't watch out."

"They'll get you all right if Jebson saw that article," said Chalmers.

The door moved ever so little—but then, perhaps it was just the cool, sweet breath of spring whispering through the window.

Lowry, swinging his stick, went out into the sunlight. It felt good to be home. The place looked and smelled good, too. For beyond the change of the seasons, there was never any difference in this town, never any real difference in the students; and when the college built a new building, why, it always looked somehow old and mellow before it was half completed. There was a sleepy sameness to the place which was soothing to one whose eyes had been so long tortured by the searing glare of spinning sun on brassy sand.

As he walked along toward his office he asked himself why he ever left this place at all. These great elms, putting forth their buds, yawning students stretched out upon the fresh green grass, colorful jackets, a mild blue sky, ancient stones and budding ivy—

For the briefest flicker he half recalled the birth of his own wanderlust. A theft in his dorm, accusation, expulsion and disgrace; and three years later—three years too late to completely remove the scar—they had finally reached him to tell him that the guilty one had been found within a week after his running away. Remembering, he again felt that seep of shame through him and the shy idea that he should apologize to the first one he met.

But it passed. It passed and the air was full of spring and hope and the smell of moist earth. Clouds, hard driven high up, occasionally flashed shadows over the pavement and lawns; the breeze close to earth frisked with the remnants of autumn, chasing leaves out of corners and across lawns and against trees, bidding them vanish and make way for a new harvest later on.

No, little ever changed in this quiet and contented mecca of education. Twenty-five years ago Franklin Lowry, his father, strolled down this same street; twenty-five years before that Ezekiel Lowry had done so. And each had done so not once but on almost every day of his mature life and then, dead, had been carried in a hearse along this way. Only James Lowry had varied such a tradition and that only slightly, but then James Lowry, in his quiet but often stubborn way, had varied many traditions. He had been the first Lowry to even start to stain that scholastic name, and he was certainly the first Lowry with the wanderlust. But then he had been a strange child; not difficult, but strange none the less.

Reared up in a great tomb of a house where no word was less than three syllables long and where the main attention paid to him was "Hush!" James Lowry had, perforce, built a universe of his own from the delicate stuff of dreams. If he cared to look in that old dean of a mansion, he knew he could find his boyhood companions tucked out of sight below the planks which covered the attic floor with indifference; Swift, Tennyson, Carroll, Verne, Dumas, Gibbon, Colonel Ingram, Shakespeare, Homer, Khayyam and the unknown creators of myth and legend of all lands had been his advisers and companions and playmates, taking him off among discards and dust and whispering strange thoughts to him, a wide-eyed child, smear-faced with jam and attic cobwebs. But, he supposed, walking down in the warmth of the new sun, he, too, would keep on walking down this street, past these stores with pennants in the windows, past these students in bright jackets, past these old elms and ancient walls; and he, too, would probably be carried in a hearse over this pavement to a resting place beside his letter-burdened forefathers.

He was fortunate, he told himself. He had a lovely lady for a wife; he had an honest and wise gentleman for a friend; he had a respected position and some small reputation as an ethnologist. What of a slight touch of malaria? That would pass. What if men did not understand so long as they were respectful and even kind? Life was good and worth the living. What more could one ask?

A group of students passed him and two, athletes from the bars on their sweater arms, touched their caps and called him "sir." A professor's wife, followed at a respectful distance by her bundle-laden maid, nodded to him with a friendly smile. A girl from the library followed him with her glance a little way and without knowing it he walked the straighter. Indeed life was good.

"Professor Lowry, sir." It was an anemic book-delver, assistant to an assistant in some department.

"Yes?"

The young man was a little out of breath and he took a moment or two, standing there and wringing a wretched cap in his hands, the better to talk clearly. "Sir, Mr. Jebson saw you pass by and sent me after you. He wants to see you, sir."

"Thank you," said Lowry, turning and retracing his steps until he came to the curving pathway which led up to the offices. He did not wonder very greatly at being summoned for he was not particularly afraid of Jebson. Presidents had come and gone at Atworthy and some of them had had peculiar ideas; that Jebson was somewhat on the stuffy side was nothing to worry about.

The girl in the outer office jumped up and opened the door for him with a muttered, "He will see you right now, sir," and Lowry went in.

Once or twice a new president had brought some furniture here and had even tried to change the appearance of this office. But the walls were older than paint and the floor had seen too many carpets pass away to shift itself much on the account of a new one. Dead men stared frostily out of frames. An eyeless bust of Cicero stood guard over a case of books which no one ever read. The chairs were so deep and so ancient that they might have been suspected of holding many a corpse that they had drowned.

Jebson was looking out of the window as though his inattention there might result in a collapse of the entire scene visible from it. He did not look around, but said, "Be seated, Lowry."

Lowry sat, regarding the president. The man was very thin and white and old, so stiff he looked more like plaster than flesh. And each passing year had dug a little deeper in the austere lines which furrowed his rather unkindly face. Jebson was motionless, for it was his pride that he had no nervous habits. Lowry waited.

Jebson, at last, opened a drawer and took out a newspaper which was partly printed in color; this he laid out before him with great care, moving his pen stand so that it would lie smoothly.

Lowry, until then, had felt peaceful. He had forgotten, completely and utterly, that article in the *Newspaper Weekly*. But even so he relaxed again, for certainly there was nothing wrong in that.

"Lowry," said Jebson, taking a sip of water which must have been white vinegar from the face he made, and then holding the glass before his face as he continued: "Lowry, we have stood a great deal from you."

Lowry sat straighter. He retreated to the far depths of himself and regarded Jebson from out the great shadows of his eyes.

"You have been needed here," said Jebson, "and yet you chose to wander in some lost and irretrievable land, consorting with the ungodly and scratching for knick-knacks like a dog looking for a bone he has buried and forgotten." Jebson was a little astonished at his own fluent flight of simile and paused. But he went on in a moment. "Atworthy has financed you when Atworthy should not have financed anything but new buildings. Atworthy was not built on nonsense."

"I have found more than enough to pay for my own expeditions," ventured Lowry. "Those money grants were refunded three years ago—"

"No mind. We are here to develop the intelligence and youth of a great nation, not to exhume the moldering bones of a heathen civilization. I am no ethnologist. I have little sympathy with ethnology. I can understand that a man might utilize such play as a hobby, but, holding as I do that man is wholly a product of his own environment, I cannot see that a study of pagan customs can furnish any true light by which to understand mankind. Very well. You know my opinions in this matter. We teach ethnology and you are the chair in anthropology and ethnology. I have no quarrel with learning of any kind, but I do quarrel with a fixation!"

"I am sorry," said Lowry.

"And I am sorry," said Jebson in the tone a master inquisitor of the Inquisition might have used condemning a prisoner to an auto-da-fé. "I refer, of course, to this article. By what leave, may I ask, was it written?"

"Why," floundered poor Lowry, "I had no idea that I was doing wrong. It seemed to me that the function of the scholar is to give his learning to those who might use it—"

"The function of the scholar has nothing to do with this, Lowry. Nothing whatever to do with this! Why, this wretched rag is a brand! It is trash and humbug! It is stuffed with lies under the name of scientific fact. And," he stated, ominously lowering his tone, "this morning I was confronted with the name of Atworthy in such a place! If a student had not brought it to me I might never have seen it at all. There it is, 'By Professor James Lowry, Ethnologist, Atworthy College.' "

"I saw no reason to sign anything else—"

"You had no right to inscribe it originally, 'Professor Lowry of Atworthy College.' It is cheap. It is a wretched attempt at notoriety. It demeans the very name and purpose of education. But then," he added with a sniff, "I suppose one cannot expect anything else from a man whose whole life has been highly irregular."

"I beg your pardon?" said Lowry.

"Oh, I have been here long enough to know the record of every man on our staff. I know you were expelled—"

"That matter was all cleared!" cried Lowry, blushing scarlet and twisted with the pain of the memory.

"Perhaps. Perhaps. But that is beside the point. This article is cheap and idiotic and by being cheap and idiotic it has demeaned the name of Atworthy." Jebson bent over it and adjusted his glasses upon the thin bridge of his nose. " 'Mankind's mental ills might in part be due to the phantoms of the witch doctors of yesterday!' Humph! 'By Professor James Lowry, Ethnologist, Atworthy College.' You will be writing about demonology next as something which one and all should believe! This is disgraceful. The entire town will be talking about it—"

Lowry had managed to control his shaking hands and now erased the quiver from his throat which sought to block his voice. "That is not an article about demonology, sir. It is an attempt to show people that their superstitions and many of their fears grew out of yesterday's erroneous beliefs. I have sought to show that demons and devils were invented to allow some cunning member of the tribe to gain control of his fellows by the process of inventing something for them to fear and then offering to act as interpreter—"

"I have read it," said Jebson. "I have read it and I can see more in it than you would like me to see. Prating of demons and devils and the placating of gods of fear— By your very inference, sir, I suddenly conceive you to mean religion itself! Next, I suppose, you will attack Christianity as an invention to overthrow the Roman capitalistic state!"

"But—" began Lowry and then, turning red again, held his tongue and retreated even further into himself.

"This wild beration of demons and devils," said Jebson, "reads like a protest of your own mind against a belief which association with the ungodly and unwashed of far lands might have instilled in you yourself. You have made yourself ludicrous. You have brought mockery upon Atworthy. I am afraid I can not readily forgive this, Lowry. In view of circumstances, I can find no saving excuse for you except that you desired money and gained it at the expense of the honor and esteem in which this institution is held. There are just two months left of this school year. We cannot dispense with you until the year is done. But after that," said Jebson, crumpling up the paper and tossing it into the wastebasket, "I am afraid you will have to look for other employment."

Lowry started up. "But—"

"With a better record, I might have forgiven. But your record has never been good, Lowry. Go back to the forgotten parts of the world, Lowry, and resume your commune with the ungodly. Good day."

Lowry walked out, not even seeing the girl who opened the doors for him; he forgot to replace his hat until he was on the walk; he had wandered several blocks before he came to himself. Dully he wondered if he had a class and then recalled that it was Saturday and that he had no Saturday classes. Vaguely he remembered having been on his way to attend a meeting or to have luncheon— no, it could not be luncheon, for it was evidently about two, according to the sun. And then the nudge of thought itself was swallowed in the wave of recollection.

He was shivering and it brought him around to thinking about himself for a moment. He mustn't shiver just because this world, for him, had come to an abrupt end; there were other colleges which might be glad to have him; there were millionaires who had offered to finance him, seeing that his traveling returned the investment and more. No, he should not feel so badly. And yet he shivered as though stripped naked to a winter's blast.

The racing clouds above darkened the street for

whole seconds at a time; but there was something dead now in the sound of last year's leaves getting chased out of corners and there was something ugly in the nakedness of these elms. He strove to locate the source of his chill.

It was Mary.

Poor Mary. She loved this world of teas and respect; she had been brought up in this town and all her memories and friendships were here. It was enough that he would be talked about. It was too much that she leave everything that was life to her. Her friends would shake their heads barely in her sight.

No, she wouldn't want to stay here, where everyone would speculate on why he was ousted, where everyone would have no more reason to ask her to teas.

And the big scholarly mansion—she loved that old place.

He failed to understand Jebson, for he was too generous to be able to run the gamut of Jebson's thought process, starting with a little man's desire to injure a big one, and envy for Lowry's rather romantic and mysterious aspect, passing through indirect insult to the college, and, finally, coming to light as a challenge to Christianity itself in some weird and half-understood way. Lowry was left floundering with only one fact on which to work: this was the culmination of a disgrace for which he had suffered acutely and innocently nearly twenty-one years before. And that pain and this pain were all entangled in his mind and driven hard home with the ache which was all through him, an ache he had forgotten was malaria.

Poor Mary.

Poor, beautiful, sweet Mary.

He had always wanted to appear grand to her, to make up somehow for being so many years older than she. And now he had brought her disgrace and separation from that which she knew best. She would take it well; she would follow him; she would be sorry and never once mention that she felt badly on her own account. Yes. Yes, she would do that, he knew. And he would not be able to prevent, nor even be able to tell her how badly he felt for her.

Again he had the recollection of having an appointment somewhere, but again he could not remember. The wind was chill now and tugged at his hat, and the clouds which swept their shadows over the pavement were darker still.

He looked about him and found that he was within sight of an old house with iron deer before it, the home of Professor Tommy Williams, who, for all his bachelorhood, maintained his family place alone.

Feeling strangely as though all had not yet happened to him and experiencing the need of shelter and company, he walked swiftly to the place and turned up the walk. The mansion seemed to repel him as he stared at it, for the two gable windows were uncommonly like a pince-nez sitting upon the nose of a moldering judge; for an instant he hesitated, almost turned around and went away.

And then he had a mental image of Tommy, the one man in this world to whom he could talk, having been the one kid with whom he had associated as a boy. But if he had come out of his boyhood with a shy reticence, Tommy had chosen another lane, for Tommy Williams was the joy of his students and the campus; he had traveled much in the old countries and therefore brought to this place an air of the cosmopolitan, a gay disregard for convention and frumpy thought. Tommy Williams loved to dabble with the exotic and fringe the forbidden, to drink special teas with weird foreign names and read cabalistic books; he told fortunes out of crystal balls at the charity affairs and loved to eye his client afterward with a sly, sideways look as though outwardly this must all be in fun, but inwardly—inwardly, mightn't it be true? Tommy was all laughter, froth and lightness, with London styles and Parisian wit, a man too clever to have any enemies—or very many friends.

No. He need not pause here on the threshold of Tommy's home. It would do him good to talk to Tommy. Tommy would cheer him and tell him that old Jebson was, at his finest, a pompous old ass. He mounted the steps and let the knocker drop.

Some dead leaves on the porch were going around in a harassed dance, making a dry and crackly music of their own; and then inanely they sped out across the lawn as though trying to catch up with a cloud shadow and so save themselves from an eventual bonfire. Nervous leaves, running away from inevitable decay, unable to cope with the rival buds which were pushing tenderly forth all unknowing that those things which fled had once been bright and green, coyly flirting with the wind. This was Lowry's thought and he did not like it, for it made him feel ancient and decayed, abandoned in favor of the fresh and green that had no flaws, who were too young to be anything but innocent; how many days would it be before another had his job? Some youthful other, preaching, perhaps, from Lowry's own books?

He dropped the knocker again, more anxious than before to be admitted to the warmths of fire and friendship; his teeth were beginning to chatter and he had a sick, all-gone sensation where his stomach should have been. Malaria?—he asked himself. Yes, he had just come from Chalmers, who had called these chills malaria. He had not two hours ago peered into a microscope where his basically stained blood was spread out so that they could see the little globes inside some of the red corpuscles. Malaria wasn't dangerous, merely uncomfortable. Yes, this must be a malarial chill and shortly it would pass.

Again he dropped the knocker and felt the sound go booming through the high-ceilinged rooms within; he wanted to go away from there, but he would not bring himself to leave just as Tommy came to the door. He shivered and turned up his collar. Very soon he would begin to burn; not unlike a leaf, he told himself. He peered through the side windows which flanked the door.

He had once more the idea that he had an engagement somewhere and pondered for an instant, trying to pull forth the reluctant fact from a stubborn recess.

No, he wouldn't keep standing here. Houses were

never locked in this town, and Tommy, even if he was not home, would welcome him eagerly when he did return; he pushed open the door and closed it behind him.

It was dim in the hall; dim with collected years and forgotten events, with crêpe long crumbled and bridal bouquets withered to dust and smoky with childish shouts and the coughing of old men. Somewhere there was a scurrying sound as though a scholarly rat had been annoyed while gnawing upon some learned tome. To the right the double doors opened portentously upon the living room, and Lowry, sensing a fire there, approached, hat in hand.

He was astonished.

Tommy Williams lay upon the sofa, one arm dangling, one foot higher than the other and both feet higher than his head; his shirt was open and he wore neither tie nor coat. For an instant Lowry thought he must be dead.

And then Tommy yawned and started a stretch; but in the middle of the action he sensed his visitor and came groggily to his feet, blinking and massaging his eyes and looking again.

"Heavens, man," said Tommy, "you gave me a start for a moment. I was sound asleep."

"I'm sorry," said Lowry, feeling unnecessary. "I thought you were gone and that I might wait until you— "

"Of course!" said Tommy. "I've slept too long any-way. What time is it?"

Lowry glanced at the great hall clock. "Five minutes after two."

"Well! That shows you what all play and no sleep will do to a fellow. Here, give me your hat and get warm by the fire. Lord, I've never seen a man look quite so blue. Is it as cold as that out?"

"I seem to be a little cold," said Lowry. "Malaria, I guess." He felt a little better—Tommy seemed so glad to see him—and he moved across the room to where two logs smoldered upon the grate. Tommy came by him and stirred them into a cheerful glow and then busied himself by the liquor cabinet, putting a drink together.

"You've got to take better care of yourself, old fel-low," said Tommy. "We've only one Professor Lowry at Atworthy and we can't run the risk of losing him. Here, take this and you'll feel better."

Lowry took the drink in his hand, but he did not immediately partake of it; he was looking around the room at the old glass-fronted cases and the china figures on the stand in the corner. When he had been little he and Tommy had never been allowed to come into this place except when there was company and they were to be presented; and then, scour-faced and feeling guilty of some crime, they had been allowed to sit stiffly in a stiffer chair and gradually relapse into suffering stupidity.

How different was that Tommy from this one! Still, there was the same winning grin, the same shining head of black hair, always slightly awry in an artistically careless way, the same classic face, startlingly pale against the blackness of the hair, the same graceful slenderness and the quick dancer movements with which he had always done things. Tommy, thought Lowry with a sudden clarity, was pretty; maybe that was what Lowry saw in him, something which complemented his own blunt ruggedness. Lowry sipped at the drink and felt the warmth of it spread pleasingly out to meet the glow from the brightly snapping flames.

Tommy was sitting on the edge of the sofa now; he always sat as though expecting to arise in another instant. He was lighting a cigarette, but he stared so long at Lowry that the match burned his fingers and he dropped it and placed the tips in his mouth. Presently he forgot about the sting and succeeded in applying the fire.

"Something is wrong, Jim."

Lowry looked at him and drank again. "It's Jebson. He found an article of mine in the *Newspaper Weekly* and he's raving mad about it."

"He'll recover," said Tommy with a rather loud laugh.

"He'll recover," said Lowry, "but just now I'm wondering if I will."

"What's this?"

"I'm being ousted at the end of the term."

"Why . . . why, the old fool! Jim, he can't mean that. It will take an order from the board—"

"He controls the board and he can do that. I've got to find another job."

"Jim! You've got to straighten this thing out. Jebson has never liked you, true, and he has muttered a great deal about you behind your back; you are too blunt, Jim. But he can't let you go this way. Why, everyone will be furious!"

They discussed the matter for a little while and then, at last, a sort of hopelessness began to enter their tones and their sentences became desultory to finally drop into a silence marked only by the occasional pop of the wood.

Tommy walked around the room with a restive grace, pausing by the whatnot stand to pick up a china elephant; tossing the fragile beast with a quick, nervous motion, he turned back to Lowry; there was a queer, strained grin on Tommy's lips but bleakness in his eyes.

"It would seem," said Tommy, "that your article has begun to catch up with you."

"That is rather obvious."

"No, no. Don't ever accuse me of being obvious, Jim. I meant the article was about demons and devils and tended to mock them as having any power—"

"Tommy," said Lowry with one of his occasional smiles, "they should put you to teaching demonology. You almost believe in it."

"When creeds fail, one must turn somewhere," said Tommy jokingly—or was it jokingly? "You say that the gods of luck are false; you wrote that it is silly to seek the aid of gods beyond the aid of the one supreme God; you said that demons and devils were the manufacture of Machiavellian witch doctors and that men could only be herded by the fear of those things they could not see; you said that men thought they found a truly good world to be an evil world in their blindness and so built a hideous structure of phantoms to people their nightmares."

"And what if I did?" said Lowry. "It is true. The world is not evil; the air and water and earth are not peopled with jealous beings anxious to undermine the happiness of man."

Tommy put the elephant back and perched himself on the edge of the couch; he was visibly agitated and kept his eyes down, pretending to inspect his immaculate nails. "No man *knows*, Jim."

Lowry rumbled out a short laugh and said, "Tell me now that you are so studied in these things that you actually credit a possibility of their existence."

"Jim, the world to you has always been a good place; that's a sort of mechanical reaction by which you like to forget all the ghastly things the world has done to you. You should be more like me, Jim. I *know* the world is an evil, capricious place and that men are basically bad and so, knowing that, I am always pleased to find some atom of goodness and only bored to see something evil. You, on the other hand, march forward relentlessly into sorrow and disappointment; to you all things are good, and when you find something which is mean and black and slimy you are revolted—and you've come to me today shivering with ague, racked by a treacherous turn done you by a man you should initially have thought good. That view of yours, Jim, will never bring you anything but misery and tears. Phantoms or not, that man is the safest who knows that all is really evil and that the air and earth and water are peopled by fantastic demons and devils who lurk to grin at and increase the sad state of man."

"And so," said Lowry, "I am to bow low to superstition and reinherit all the gloomy thoughts of my benighted ancestors. Devil take your devils, Tommy Williams, for I'll have nothing of them."

"But it would appear," said Tommy in a quiet, even, ominous way, "that they will have something of you."

"How can you arrive at that?"

"It would appear," said Tommy, "that the devils and demons have won their first round."

"Bah," said Lowry, but a chill coursed through him.

"You say they do not exist, in an article in the *Newspaper Weekly*. That same article arouses the rage of a vindictive fool and thereby causes your scheduled dismissal from Atworthy."

"Nonsense," said Lowry, but less briskly.

"Be nice and say the world is an evil place, filled with evil spirits. Be nice and forget your knightly manner. And now be nice and go home and fill yourself with quinine and rest."

"And I came to you," said Lowry with a smile, "for solace."

"To solace is to lie," said Tommy. "I gave you something better than that."

"Devils and demons?"

"Wisdom."

Lowry walked slowly into the hall, the chill making it difficult for him to speak clearly. Confound it, he was certain that he had an appointment somewhere this afternoon. He could almost recall the time as a quarter to three and the old clock was chiming that now. He reached toward the rack where his hat lay in a thick mass of coats and canes.

CHAPTER

2

And a white shape was moving slowly toward him on soundless feet and a white face gleamed dully above a glittering knife. Nearer and nearer—

It was dusk, at the twilight's end; all along the street windows were lighted and people could be seen through some of them, people with talk and food in their mouths; the wind had picked up along the earth and brought a great gout of white scurrying out of the dark—a newspaper. High above, a cool moon looked out now and then through rifts of anxiously fleeing clouds, and now and again a star blinked briefly beyond the torn masses of blue and black and silver.

Where was he?

The street sign said Elm and Locust Avenues, which meant that he was only half a block from Tommy's house and about a block from his own. He looked worriedly at his watch by the sphere of yellow in the middle of the street and found that it was a quarter to seven.

A quarter to seven!

The chill took him and his teeth castaneted briefly until he made his jaw relax. He felt for his hat, but it was gone; he felt panicky about the loss of his hat and cast anxiously about to see if it lay anywhere near.

A group of students strolled by; a girl flattered by the teasing of the three boys about her; one of them nodded respectfully to Lowry.

A quarter to three.

A quarter to seven.

Four hours!

Where had he been?

Tommy's. That was it. Tommy's. But he had left there at a quarter to three. And it was now a quarter to seven.

Four hours!

He had never been really drunk in his whole life, but he knew that when one drank indiscreetly there usually followed a thick head and a raw stomach; and as nearly as he could remember he had had only that one drink at Tommy's. And certainly one drink was not enough to blank his mind.

It was horrible, having lost four hours; but just why it was horrible he could not understand.

Where had he gone?

Had he seen anyone?

Would somebody come up to him on the morrow and say, "That was a fine talk you gave at the club, Professor Lowry"?

It wasn't malaria. Malaria in its original state might knock a man out, but even in delirium a man knew where he was, and he certainly had no symptoms of having been delirious. No, he hadn't been drunk and it wasn't malaria.

He began to walk rapidly toward his home. He had a gnawing ache inside him which he could not define, and he carried along that miserable sensation of near-memory which goes with words which refuse to come but halfway into consciousness; if he only tried a little harder he would know where he had been.

The night was ominous to him and it was all that he could do to keep his pace sane; every tree and bush was a lurking shape which might at any moment materialize into—into— In the name of God, what was wrong with him? Could it be that he was afraid of the dark?

Eagerly he turned into his own walk. For all that he could see, the ancient mansion slept, holding deep shadows close to it like its memories of a lost youth.

He halted for a moment at the foot of the steps, wondering a little that he saw no light in the front of the house; but then perhaps Mary had grown alarmed at his failure to come home and had gone to his office—no, she would have phoned. A clamoring alarm began to go within him.

Abruptly a shriek stabbed from the blackness:

"Jim! Oh, my God! Jim!"

He vaulted the steps and nearly broke down the door as he entered; for a moment he paused, irresolute, in the hall, casting madly about him, straining to catch the sound of Mary's voice again.

There was nothing but silence and memory in this house.

He leaped up the wide stairway to the second floor, throwing on lights with hungry fingers as he went. He glanced into all the rooms on the second floor without result and sprang up the narrow débris-strewn stairs to the attic. It was dismal here and the wind was moaning about the old tower and trunks crouched like black beasts in the gloom; he lighted a match and the old familiar shapes leaped up to reassure him. She was not here!

Tremblingly he made his way down, to again examine

the rooms of the second floor. He was beginning to feel sick at his stomach and his blood was two sledge hammers knocking out his temples from within. He had lighted everything as he had come up, and the light itself seemed harsh to him, harsh and unkindly in that it revealed an empty house.

Could she have gone next door?

Was there a dinner somewhere that she had had to attend without him? Yes, that must be it. A note somewhere, probably beside his chair, telling him to hurry and dress and stop disgracing them.

On the first floor again he searched avidly for the note, beside his chair, on the dining-room table, in the kitchen, on his study desk, on the mantelpiece— No, there wasn't any note.

He sank down on the couch in his study and cupped his face in his hands; he tried to order himself and stop quivering; he tried to fight down the nausea which was, he knew, all terror. Why was he allowing himself to become so upset? She must not have gone very far, and if she had not left a note, why then she intended to be back shortly.

Nothing could happen to anyone in this lazy, monotonous town.

Her absence made him feel acutely what life would mean without her. He had been a beast, leaving her and running away to far lands, leaving her to this lonely old place and the questionable kindness of faculty friends. Life without her would be an endless succession of purposeless days lived with a heavy hopelessness.

For minutes he sat there, trying to calm himself, trying to tell himself that there was nothing wrong, and after a little he did succeed in inducing a state of mind which, if not comfortable, at least allowed him to stop shivering

The outer door slammed and quick footsteps sounded in the hall. Lowry leaped up and ran to the door.

She was hanging up her new fur wrap.

"Mary!"

She looked at him in surprise, so much had he put into the word.

"There you are, Jim Lowry! You vagabond! Where were you all this time?"

But he wasn't listening to her; his arms were almost crushing her and he was laughing with happiness. She laughed with him, even though he was completely ruining the set of her hair and crumpling the snowy collar of her dress.

"You're beautiful," said Lowry. "You're lovely and wonderful and grand and if I didn't have you I would walk right out and step over a cliff."

"You better not."

"You're the only woman in the world. You're sweet and loyal and good!"

Mary's face was glowing and her eyes, when she pushed him back a little to look up at him, were gentle. "You're an old bear, Jim. Now account for yourself. Where have you been?"

"Why—" and he stopped, feeling very uneasy. "I don't know, Mary."

"Let me smell your breath."

"I wasn't drunk."

"But you're shivering. Jim! Have you gotten malaria again? And here you are walking around when you should be in bed—"

"No. I'm all right. Really, I'm all right, Mary. Where were you?"

"Out looking for you."

"I'm sorry I worried you."

She shrugged. "Worry me a little now and then and I'll know how much I worship you. But here we are gabbing and you haven't had anything to eat. I'll get you something immediately."

"No! I'll get it. Look. You just sit down there by the fire and I'll light it and—"

"Nonsense."

"You do as I tell you. You sit there where I can look at you and be your most beautiful and I'll rustle up my chow. Now don't argue with me."

She smiled as he forced her down into the chair and giggled at him when he dropped the sticks he had picked up from the basket. "Clumsy old bear."

He got the fire going and then, putting out his hand as a protest against her moving, he sped through the dining room and into the kitchen, where he hurriedly threw together a sandwich from yesterday's roast beef and poured himself a glass of milk. He was so frightened that she would be gone before he could get back that he resisted all impulse to make coffee.

Presently he was again in the living room, sighing in relief that she was still there. He sat down on the lounge opposite from her and held the sandwich in front of his face for a full minute, just looking at her.

"Go on and eat," said Mary. "I'm no good at all to let you sup on cold food."

"No, no! I won't have you do a thing. Just sit there and be beautiful." He ate slowly, relaxing little by little until he was half-sprawled on the lounge. And then a thought brought him upright again. "When I came in here I heard screams."

"Screams?"

"Certainly. You sounded like you were calling to me."

"Must be the Allison radio. Those kids can find the most awful programs and they haven't the least idea of tuning them down. The whole family must be deaf."

"Yes, I guess you are right. But it gave me an awful scare." He relaxed again and just looked at her.

She had very provocative eyes, dark and languorous, so that when she gave him a slow look he could feel little tingles of pleasure go through him. What a fool he was to go away from her! She was so young and so lovely— He wondered what she had ever seen in an old fool like himself. Of course, there were only about ten years between them and he had lived outdoors so much that he didn't look so very much over thirty-one or thirty-two. Still, when he sat like this, studying her sweet face and the delicate rondures of her body and seeing the play of firelight in her dark hair and feeling the caress of her eyes, he could not wholly understand why she had ever begun to love him at all; Mary, who could have had her choice from fifty men, who had even been courted by Tommy Williams— What did she see in a burly, clumsy, granite-being like himself? For a moment he was panicky at the thought that some day she might grow tired of his silences, his usual lack of demonstrativeness, his long absences—

"Mary—"

"Yes, Jim?"

"Mary, do you love me a little bit?"

"A lot more than a little bit, Jim Lowry."

"Mary—"

"Yes?"

"Tommy once asked you to marry him, didn't he?"

A slight displeasure crossed her face. "Any man that could carry on an affair with a student and still ask me to marry him— Jim, don't be jealous again; I thought we had put all that away long ago."

"But you married me instead."

"You're strong and powerful and everything a woman wants in a man, Jim. Women find beauty in men only when they find strength; there's something wrong with a woman, Jim, when she falls in love with a fellow because he is pretty."

"Thank you, Mary."

"And now, Mr. Lowry, I think you had better get yourself to bed before you fall asleep on that couch."

"Just a little longer."

"No!" She got up and pulled him to his feet. "You're half on fire and half frozen, and when you get these attacks the best thing for you is bed. I couldn't ever see what pleasure a man could get out of wandering off to some land just so he could roast in the sun and let a bug bite him. To bed with you, Mr. Lowry."

He let her force him up the stairs and into his room and then he gave her a long kiss and a hug sufficient to break her ribs before he let her return to the living room.

He felt very comfortable inside as he undressed and was almost on the verge of singing something as he hung up his suit when he noticed a large tear on the collar. He inspected it more closely. Yes, there were other tears and the cloth was all wrinkled and stiff in spots as if from mud. Why, good grief! The suit was ruined! He puzzled over it and then, in disgust for having destroyed good English tweeds, he crammed jacket and trousers into the bottom of a clothes hamper.

As he got into his pajamas he mused over what a lovely person Mary really was. She hadn't called his attention to it and yet he must have looked a perfect wreck.

He washed his hands and face in an absent sort of way, musing over how he could have wrecked his suit. He dried himself upon a large bath towel and was about to slip on his pajama coat when he was shocked to see something which looked like a brand upon his forearm.

It was not very large and there was no pain in it;

interested, he held his arm closer to the light. The thing was scarlet! A scarlet mark not unlike a tattoo. And what a strange shape it had, like the footpads of a small dog; one, two, three, four—four little pads, as though a small animal had walked there. But there were few dogs that small. More like a rabbit—

"Strange," he told himself.

He went into his room and turned out the light. "Strange." He eased in between the covers and plumped up his pillow. A mark like the footprint of a rabbit. How could he have torn his suit and stained it with mud? What could have put this stamp upon his arm? A chill came over him and he found it difficult to stop his jaw muscles from contracting.

The cool moon, blanked out for seconds by the racing clouds, laid a window pattern across the foot of his bed. He flung the covers back, annoyed that he had forgotten to open the window, and raised the sash. An icy belt was thrown about him by the wind and he threw himself hurriedly back between the covers.

Well, tomorrow was quite another day, and when the sun came he would feel better; still, malaria had never given him this sick feeling in his stomach.

The cool moon's light was blue and the wind found a crack under the door and began to moan a dismal dirge; the sound was not constant, but built slowly from a whisper into a round groan and then into a shriek, finally dying again into a sigh. And lying there Jim Lowry thought there was a voice in it; he twisted about and attempted to cover up his right ear, burrowing his left in the pillow.

The wind was whimpering and every few seconds it would weep, "Where?" And then it would mutter out and grumble and come up again as though tiptoeing to his bedside to cry, "Why?"

Jim Lowry turned over and again pulled the covers down tight against his ear.

"Where?"

A whimpering complaint.

"Why?"

The window rattled furiously as though something was trying to get in; with tingling skin, Lowry came up on his elbow and stared at the pattern of light. But the cool moon's light was only marred by the speeding clouds. Again the window was beaten and again there was only moonlight.

"I'm a fool," said Lowry, pulling up the covers again.

A sigh.

"Why?"

A whimpering complaint.

"Where?"

The curtain began to beat against the glass and Lowry flung out to raise it all the way so that it could not move. But the string and disk kept striking against the pane and he had to locate a pin so that he could secure them.

"I'm a fool," said Lowry.

He had listened to drums off somewhere in the black. He had slid into dark caverns to feel tarantulas and snakes running over or striking his boots; he had once awakened with a moccasin slithering out from under his top blanket; he had mocked at curses; he had once taken a cane knife away from an infuriated and drunken native—

A sigh.

"Why?"

A whimpering complaint.

"Where?"

Fear's sadistic fingers reached in and found his heart and aped its regular rhythm to send his blood coursing in his throat. Just the moan of the wind under a door and the protest of the curtains and the rattle of the sash and the moon's cold blue light upon the bottom of his bed—

The door opened slowly and the curtain streamed straight out as the wind leaped into the room from the window. The door banged and the wall shivered. And a white shape was moving slowly toward him on soundless feet and a white face gleamed dully above a glittering knife. Nearer and nearer—

Lowry sprang savagely at it and knocked the knife away.

But it was Mary.

Mary stood there looking at him in hurt amazement, her hand empty but still upheld. "Jim!"

He was shaking with horror at the thought he might have hurt her; weakly he sank upon the edge of the bed, and yet there was relief in him, too. A broken glass lay upon the rug when she turned on the light and a white pool of warm milk steamed in the cold air. She held her hand behind her and, with sudden suspicion, he dragged it forth. He had struck the glass so hard that it had cut her.

He pulled her small hand to the light and anxiously extracted a broken fragment from the cut and then applied his lips to it to make it bleed more freely. He opened a drawer and took out his expedition first-aid kit and found some antiseptic and bandages. She seemed to be far more anxious about him than about her hand.

"Mary."

"Yes?"

He pulled her down to the edge of the bed and threw part of the spread about her shoulders.

"Mary, something awful has happened to me. I didn't tell you. There are two things I didn't tell you. Jebson found that *Newspaper Weekly* article and at the end of this term I am going to be dismissed. We . . . we'll have to leave Atworthy."

"Is that all, Jim? You know that I don't care about this place; anywhere you go, I'll go." She was almost laughing. "I guess you'll have to drag me along, no matter how deep the jungles are, Jim."

"Yes. You can go with me, Mary. I was a fool never to have allowed it before. You must have been terribly lonely here."

"I am always lonely without you, Jim."

41

He kissed her and felt that this must be the way a priest might feel touching the foot of his goddess.

"And the other thing, Jim?"

"I . . . I don't know, Mary. I have no idea where I was between a quarter of three and a quarter of seven. Four hours gone out of my life. I wasn't drunk. I wasn't delirious. Four hours, Mary."

"Maybe you fell and struck something."

"But there is no bruise."

"Maybe you don't know all there is to know about malaria."

"If it blacks out a mind, then it is so serious that the patient isn't going to feel as well as I do now. No, Mary. It . . . it was something else. Tommy and I were talking about demons and devils and . . . and he said that maybe I should not have attacked them in that article. He said they might be trying . . . well— The world *is* a good place, Mary. It isn't filled with evil things. Man has no reason to walk in the shadow of dread because of phantoms."

"Of course he hasn't, Jim. Tomorrow you may find out what happened. It might be something perfectly innocent."

"You think so, Mary?"

"Certainly. Now you lie down there and get some sleep."

"But—"

"Yes, Jim?"

"I feel . . . well . . . I feel as though something horrible had happened to me and that . . . that something even more horrible is going to happen soon. I don't know what it is. If I could only find out!"

"Lie down and sleep, Jim."

"No. No, I can't sleep. I am going out and walk and maybe the exercise will clear my head and I'll remember—"

"But you are ill!"

"I can't lie here any longer. I can't stay still!"

He put down the window and began to dress. She watched him resignedly as he slipped into a jacket.

"You won't be gone very long?"

"Only half an hour or so. I feel I must walk or explode. But don't disturb yourself on my account. Go to sleep."

"It's nearly midnight."

"I feel—" He stopped, beginning again with a different tone. "This afternoon I felt I had an appointment somewhere at a quarter to three. Maybe I went somewhere— No. I don't know where I went or what I did. No. I don't know! Mary."

"Yes, Jim?"

"You're all right?"

"Of course I'm all right."

He buttoned up his topcoat and bent over and kissed her. "I'll be back in half an hour. I feel I . . . well, I've just got to walk, that's all. Good night."

"Good night, Jim."

CHAPTER

3

"*Well, now, James Lowry, that's a very silly thing to do, to do, to do. To lose your hat. You are old enough to know better, and your head is big enough to keep a hat on. But that isn't all you've lost, James Lowry.*"

The night was clean and clear and, as he poised for a moment on top of the steps, the smell of fresh earth and growing things came to him and reawakened his memories. It was the kind of night that makes a child want to run and run forever out across the field, to feel the earth fly from beneath his feet, driven by the incomprehensible joy of just being alive. On such a night he and Tommy had once visited a cave a mile out of town which was supposed to be haunted and had succeeded in frightening themselves out of their wits by beholding a white shape which had turned out to be an old and lonely horse. The memory of it revived Lowry: Tommy's fantastic imagination and his glib tongue!

And how Tommy loved to devil his slower and more practical friend; that had just been devilment today. Witches and spooks and old wives' tales, devils and demons and black magic. How Tommy, who believed in nothing, liked to pretend to beliefs which would shock people! How he adored practically knocking his students out of their seats by leaning over his desk and saying, in a mysterious voice, "To be polite, we call this psychology, but, in reality, you know and I know that we are studying the black goblins and fiendish ghouls which lie in pretended slumber just out of sight of our conscious minds." How he loved such simile! Of course, what he said was true, absolutely true, but Tommy had to choose that way of putting it; it was such a dull world, so drab; why not enliven it a little and stick pins into people's imaginations? Indeed, dear Tommy, why not?

The top of his head was cold and he reached up to

discover that he had forgotten his hat, and, discovering that, remembered that he had lost it. Because his gear was mainly tropical he had only one felt hat, and one did not walk around Atworthy in a solar topi; not Atworthy! The loss of it troubled him. And his best tweed ruined beyond repair! But then his hat had his name in the band, being a good hat, and some student would find it where the wind had taken it and return it to the dean's office— Still, there was something wrong in that; there was a deeper significance to having lost his hat, something actually symbolic of his lost four hours. Part of him was gone; four hours had been snatched ruthlessly from his life and with them had gone a felt hat. It struck him that if he could find the hat he could also find the four hours. Strange indeed that anything should so perplex him, the man whom little had perplexed.

Four hours gone.

His hat gone.

He had the uneasy feeling that he ought to walk along the street toward Tommy's and see if the hat was there under a bush; it seemed a shame to leave a good hat on some lawn; it might rain.

Yes, most certainly, he had better find that hat.

He started down the steps to the walk, glancing up at the hurrying fleece between earth and the moon. He had been down these steps thousands of times; when he reached the "bottom" he almost broke his leg on an *extra step*.

He stared at his feet and hastily backed up, swiftly to discover that he could *not* retreat. He almost fell over backward into space! There were no steps above him, only a descent of them below him. Glassy-eyed he looked down the flight, trying to take in such a length of steps. Now and then they faded a little as they went through a dark mist, but there was no clue whatever of what might lie waiting at the bottom.

He looked anxiously overhead and was relieved to find that the moon was still there; he was standing so that his eyes were above the level of the yard and he felt that he could reach over to the indefinite rim and somehow pull himself out. He reached, but the rim jerked away from him and he almost fell. Breathless, he stared down the flight to mystery. The moon, the steps, and no connection between himself and the porch.

Somewhere he thought he heard a tinkle of laughter and glared about, but it was evidently nothing more than a set of Japanese wind chimes on the porch. Somehow he knew that he dared not reach the bottom, that he had not sanity enough to face the awful thing which waited there. But then, all he had to do was descend two more steps and he would be able to reach up to the rim and haul himself forth. He descended; the rim retreated. That was no way to go about it, he told himself, glancing at his empty hands. He would back up—

Again he almost went over backward into a void! The two steps he had descended had vanished away from his very heels.

There was that laughter again—no, just the sweet chording of the wind chimes.

He peered down the angle of the flight, through the strata of dark mist, into a well of ink. Wait. Yes, there was a door down there, on the side of the flight, not thirty steps below him. That door must lead out and up again; the very least he could do would be to chance it. He went down, pausing once and glancing over his shoulder. How odd that these steps should cease to exist as soon as he passed along them! For there was now nothing but a void between himself and the front of his house; he could still see the lights shining up there. What would Mary think—

"Jim! Jim, you forgot your hat!"

He whirled and stared up. There was Mary on the porch, staring down into the cavity which had been a walk.

"Jim!" She had seen the hole now.

"I'm down here, Mary. Don't come down. I'll be up in a moment. It's all right."

The moonlight was too dim for him to see the expression on her face. Poor thing, she was probably scared to death.

"Jim! Oh, my God! Jim!"

Wasn't his voice reaching her? "I'm all right, Mary! I'll be back as soon as I reach this door!" Poor kid.

She was starting down the steps, and he cupped his hands to shout a warning at her. She could do nothing more than step out into space! "Stop, Mary! *Stop!*"

There was a peal of thunder and the earth rolled

together over his head, vanishing the moonlight, throwing the whole flight into complete blackness.

He stood there trembling, gripping the rough, earthy wall.

From far, far off he heard the cry, dwindling into nothing, "Jim! Oh, my God! Jim!" Then it came again as the merest whisper. And finally once more, as soundless as a memory.

She was all right, he told himself with fury. She was all right. The hole had closed before she had come down to it, and now the trap up there was thickening and making it impossible for her voice to get through. But he felt, somehow, that it was all wrong. That she wasn't up there now. He began to quiver and feel sick, and his head spun until he was certain that he would pitch forward and go tumbling forever into the mystery which reached up from the bottom—the bottom he dared not approach.

Well, there was a door ahead of him. He couldn't stand here whimpering like a kid and expect to get out of this place. He'd seen the door and he'd find it. He groped down, feeling for each step with a cautious foot and discovering that their spacing was not even, some of them dropping a yard and others only an inch. The wall, too, had changed character under his hands, for now it was slimy and cold, as though water had seeped down from above for ages, wearing the stone smooth and glossing it with moss. Somewhere water was dripping slowly, one drop at a time, frighteningly loud in the corpse-quietness of this place.

He'd been in worse, he told himself. But it was funny, living in that house all those years without ever suspecting the existence of such a flight at the very bottom of his front steps.

What was he doing here, anyhow? He'd told himself that he had to find something—

Four hours in his life.

A felt hat.

Where the devil was that door? He had come thirty steps and his questing hands had yet to find it. Maybe he could back up now, but when he tried that he found that the steps had kept on vanishing as he went over them. If he had passed the door he could never get back to it now! A panic shook him for a moment. Maybe the door had been on the other side of the stairs! Maybe he had gone by it altogether! Maybe he would have to go down—all the way down to— To what?

Something sticky and warm drifted by his cheek and he recognized it as probably being a stratum of mist; but what strange mist it was! Warm and fibrous, and even vibrant, as though it was alive! He strung several strands of it with his hands, and then, as though he had caught a snake, it wriggled and was gone.

He rubbed his palms against his coat, trying to rid them of the tingling feeling. He stepped lower, and now the mist was clinging to him like cobwebs, sticking to his cheeks and tangling about his shoulders.

Somewhere he heard a faint call. "Jim! Jim Lowry!"

He tried to surge toward it, but the mist held him with invisible, sticky fingers.

"Jim Lowry!"

What an empty voice!

With all his strength he tore at the mist, expecting it to string out and tear away; but instead, it was like being released all at once, and he nearly fell down the steps he could not see. Again he sought the wall and felt his way along, now and again hopeful that the steps above had not vanished, but finding always that they had. There must be a door somewhere!

The shock of light blinded him.

He was standing on what seemed to be solid earth, but there was no sun—only light, blinding and harsh. Seared earth, all red and raw, stretched away for a little distance on every side; great gashes had been washed out of gratey stone.

A small boy sat unconcernedly upon a small rock and dug his initials out of the stony earth. He was whistling a nonsensical air, badly off key, with *whooshes* now and then creeping out with his whistle. He pulled his straw hat sideways and glanced at Lowry.

"Hello."

"Hello," said Lowry.

"You ain't got any hat on," said the boy.

"No. So I haven't."

"And your hands are dirty," said the boy, returning to his aimless task.

"What's your name?" said Lowry.

"What's yours?" said the boy.

"Mine's Jim."

"That's funny. Mine's Jim, too. Only it's really James, you know. Looking for something?"

"Well—yes. My hat."

"I saw a hat."

"Did you? Where?"

Solemnly the boy said, "On my father's head." He gave vent to a wild peal of laughter at his joke. Then he reached into his pocket. "Want to see something?"

"Why, I suppose so. If it's worth seeing."

The boy took out a rabbit's foot and held it admiringly toward Lowry. Then there was just a rabbit's foot hanging there, and darkness reached in from the outskirts of the land and swallowed even that. Lowry took a step and again almost fell down the stairs. He inched his way along; water was dripping somewhere; the steps were more and more worn with age; from the moss on them it was doubtful if many had passed this way.

Below he saw a dull gleam which seemed to emanate from a side entrance. Well! There was a door down there, after all! Why hadn't he walked off into the harsh red land and so found his way back to the top again! But, never mind, here was a door ahead of him, and a door meant egress from these stairs. Thank God he did not have to go to the bottom!

Mist swirled briefly and the door was faded out, but in a moment it had again appeared, clearer than before except that it was now closed and the light came from an indefinable source on the stairs themselves. He was not particularly frightened now, for he was intent upon a certain thing: he knew that somewhere he would find his hat and the four hours. He felt he should have asked the boy.

When he stood before the door he breathed heavily with relief. Once away from these steps he knew he would feel better. He tried the handle, but the portal was locked from within, and there was no sign of a knocker. He bent over to squint through the keyhole, but there was no keyhole. He straightened up and was not surprised to discover that a knocker had appeared before him; the thing was a verdigris-stained head of a woman out of whose head grew snakes, the Medusa. He dropped it, and the sound went bouncing from wall to wall down the steps as though a stone was falling. He waited a long while before he heard any sound from within, but just as he was about to raise the knocker again there came out a grating of rusty bars which were being removed and then the latch rattled and the door swung wide and the acrid smell of burning herbs and a thick, unclean cloud of darkness rolled from the place; two bats squeaked as they flew forth, hitting Lowry with a soft, skin wing. The smell of the place and the smoke got into his eyes so that he could not clearly see the woman; he had an impression of a wasted face and yellow teeth all broken and awry, of tangled, colorless hair and eyes like holes in a skull.

"Mother, I would like to leave these stairs," said Lowry.

"Mother? Oh, so you are polite tonight, James Lowry. So you'd like to flatter me into thinking you are really going to stand there and try to come in. Hah-hah! No, you don't, James Lowry."

"Wait, mother, I don't know how you know my name, for I have never been here before, but—"

"You've been on these stairs before. I never forget a face. But now you are coming down, and then you were going up, and your name was not James Lowry, and every time you went up another step you would kick away the one below, and when you came here you laughed at me and had me whipped and spat upon my face! I never forget!"

"That is not true!"

"It will do until there's something that *is* true in this place. And now I suppose you want your hat."

"Yes. Yes, that's it. My hat. But how did you know that I was looking—"

"How do I know anything? Hah-hah. He's lost his hat. It went like a bat. Now what do you think of that? He's lost his hat! Well, now, James Lowry, that's a very silly thing to do, to do, to do. To lose your hat. You are old enough to know better, and your head is big enough to keep a hat on. But that isn't all you've lost, James Lowry."

"Why—no, it isn't."

"You've lost four hours, just like that! Four whole hours and your hat. Want advice?"

"If you please, mother, can't we come in off these *stairs?*"

"You can't leave them. You walked up them, and now you'll walk down them all the way to the bottom. You must do it, that's all there is to it. You can sag and drag and gag and wag, but you've got to go to the bottom. All the way down. All the way down. All the way, way, way, way, way, way, way down! *Down! Down! Down!* Want some advice?"

"If you please."

"Then give me your pocket handkerchief."

He gave it to her, and she violently blew her nose upon it and threw it out into the darkness. In a moment one of the bats came back, bringing it. She threw it away and the other bat came back.

"Runaways!" she scolded them. "Want some advice, James Lowry?"

"Please, mother."

"Don't try to find your hat."

"Why not, mother?"

"*Because if you find your hat you'll find your four hours, and if you find your four hours then you will die!*"

Lowry blinked at her as she stuffed the pocket handkerchief into his coat and reached out, talon-fingered, toward his throat. But though he felt the bite of her nails, she was only straightening his tie.

"Want advice, James Lowry?"

"Yes, mother."

"Hats are hats and cats are cats, and when the birds sing there is something awry in the world. Bats are bats and hats are hats, and when it is spring the world is only bracing itself for another death. Rats are rats and hats are hats, and if you can't walk faster then you'll never be a master. You have a kind face, James Lowry. Want some advice?"

"Yes, mother."

"Go on down the stairs and you'll meet a man. If you are bound to die, then ask him where you lost your hat."

"He'll tell me?"

"Maybe he will and maybe he won't. Bats are hats are rats are cats are hats and there is no soup deep enough to drown."

"Drown what, mother?"

"Why, to drown, that's all! You have a kind face, James Lowry."

"Thank you, mother."

"And then you'll meet another man after you meet the first man. But they aren't men, either of them. They're ideas. And the first man will tell you that you are about to meet the second man, and then the second man will tell you that you have to go on down to the foot of the stairs. All the way to the bottom. Down, down, down—"

"Where is the bottom, mother?"

"At the top, of course. Hats lead to bats, lead to cats, lead to rats. Rats are hungry, James Lowry. Rats will eat you, James Lowry. Hats, you came here to bats, you go on to cats, you get eaten by the rats. Do you still want to find your hat?"

"Please, mother."

"Oh, what a contrary, stubborn, bullheaded, witless, rotten, thoughtless, bestial, wicked, heartless, contrary, stubborn, bullheaded, witless, rotten— Do you still want to find your hat, James Lowry?"

"Yes, mother."

"You don't believe in demons and devils?"

"No, mother."

"You *still* don't believe in demons or devils?"

"No, mother."

"Then look behind you, James Lowry."

He whirled.

But there was only darkness.

There was the sound of a slamming door. Far away a voice cried, "Jim! Jim Lowry!"

When he felt of the place where the door had been, for it was inky dark once more, he could find nothing but the wall. He groped upward, but the steps were gone. He groped downward and the voice, clearer now, was calling, "Jim! Jim Lowry!"

Step by step, sometimes an inch and sometimes a yard, sometimes slanting to the right, sometimes level and sometimes to the left, but always the opposite direction from what they first appeared. Another stratum of mist, white this time, curling smokily about him; it was full of something that stung his throat, but something, too, which made him walk with less fear and a straighter back.

"Jim! Jim Lowry!"

It was quite close now; it sounded hollow, as though it was being brayed by a town crier into an echo-box. There wasn't much interest in it any more than there is interest in the voice of a train caller bidding the commuters to pack into the 5:15.

"Oh, Jim! Jim Lowry!"

Paging Mr. Lowry. Paging Mr. Lowry.

The white mist was clearing as he came down into its lower levels, and he could see the stairs now. They had changed; they were clean and dry and made of polished marble, and they had an elaborately carved railing which, after the stone, was very soothing to his touch. It seemed that this case was winding a little, and that just below there was a great hall hung in banners with half a hundred guests about a board—but he did not feel that he should go near the guests. A big Great Dane came bounding up to him and almost knocked him down, and then, as though it had made a mistake, gave a sniff and walked, stiff-legged, away. Lowry kept on going down the steps.

"Jim! Jim Lowry!"

He was on a landing stage, and something had happened to the guests in the great hall, though he knew they were quite near. To his right hung a gold-and-white tapestry depicting combat in the lists, and to his left stood a stand full of lances, above which hung a sword plaque and a shield with three rampant lions upon it.

A hand tapped him on the shoulder and he snapped around to find a tall knight in full armor, made taller by the waving white plume of his visored helmet, the visor of which was down.

"James Lowry?"

"Yes?"

"Are you sure you are Jim Lowry?"

"Yes."

"Then why answer to the name of James? Never mind, we won't quibble. You know me?"

"I am sorry that I can't seem to place you. Your helmet visor is down, you know, and you are all cased in steel—"

"Well, well, old fellow, we won't equivocate about a visor now, will we? We are both gentlemen, and so there is no reason to quarrel, is there? Especially about a little thing like a visor. You think you are dreaming, don't you?"

"Why, no. I didn't exactly—"

"That's it. You are not dreaming. See, I'll pinch you." And he did, and nodded sagely when Lowry jerked away. "You are not dreaming, and this is all perfectly real. If you don't believe it yet, then look at the mark these steel fingers made."

Lowry glanced at the back of his hand and saw that it was bruised and bleeding.

"Now about this hat," said the knight. "You're bound to find it?"

"Certainly."

"It was only worth a few dollars, you know. And believe me, old man, what are a few dollars compared to the value of your own life?"

"What does my life have to do with a hat?"

"Oh, now I say, old fellow, didn't you hear the old mother tell you that if you found the hat you found the four hours, and that if you found the four hours you lost your life? Now let's look at this thing sagely, eh? Let's examine it in the light of cold and dispassionate reasoning. A hat is worth perhaps ten dollars. During the remaining thirty-five years of your life you will probably make a hundred and fifty thousand dollars at, say, forty-five hundred dollars a year. Now is that anything to exchange for a ten-dollar bill?"

"Well-l-l—no-o-o."

"All right, old fellow, I'm glad you see my point. Now let us probe more deeply into this problem. You are a very intelligent man. You have lost four hours. In the thirty-five years you may yet live there will be exactly three hundred and five thousand, four hundred and forty hours. Is that time sufficient to outweigh a perfectly stupid period like four hours?"

"No—but—"

"Ah, so we must still argue about this some more. You are bound to find your hat, eh?"

"I would like to."

"And you won't worry if you find your hat and then find the four hours—for they are right there side by side?"

"Well—"

"Now! I thought you'd weaken after a while. Find your hat, find four hours, find death. That's the way it will run. Hats are too numerous for you to go scrambling around looking for just one."

"I'll . . . I'll think it over."

"Don't do that. You should be convinced right here and now that it is no use finding the hat. And forget the four hours. Forget them quite completely."

"Maybe—" ventured Lowry, "maybe you can tell me what *did* happen in those four hours."

"Oh, now, come, old fellow! I tell you that if you find out you will surely die, and you ask me point-blank to tell you. And here I am trying to *save* you, not destroy you."

"You can't even give me a hint?"

"Why should I?"

"Was it that article—"

"Tut, tut, Jim Lowry. Don't try to worm it out of me, for I have no reason to wish you dead. In fact, I think you are a swell fellow, a veritable prince and the best there is. Now you just go on down—"

"Was it malaria?"

"Tut, tut."

"Was it the drink?"

"Hush, now."

"Was it—"

"I said to be quiet!" roared the knight. "If you are so determined to learn, you go on down those steps and you'll come to a man. That's all I'll say. You'll come to a man."

"Thank you," said Lowry. "And now, would you mind telling me your name?"

"Name? Why should I have a name? I am a knight, and I am full of ideals."

"But if I see you again I won't recognize you."

"I said I am full of ideals!"

"Well, what difference does that make? I am full of ideals, too." He reached out and started to raise the fellow's visor. The knight did not jerk away, but stood quite still.

The visor went up.

The suit was empty!

And there was darkness.

After a little while Lowry made another attempt to go up, but again it was futile; he almost fell through the void above him. He stood still, shivering. Did—did he have to go *down there*, after all? Down to— Swiftly he shook off the wild craving to scream. He grew calm.

There was something a little different about these steps, he found; they gave out another sound, a hollow sound, as though they were built of lumber; and unlike the others which had been above, these were regular. After a very short descent he almost fell trying to reach a step which was seemingly solid earth. Yes. He was on a flat expanse of earth! He could see nothing—

Suddenly he turned and felt for the bottom step. It was still there. The one above it was still there. The one above that was still there. Maybe the stairs were all there once more! Perhaps he could again regain the top! But again he stumbled, for where there had been a landing of marble there was now a platform of wood with a railing about it and further ascent was impossible. He went down the steps again to the flat expanse of earth.

He had not seen the fellow before, mainly because the fellow was all dressed in black. All in black. He wore a black slouch hat with a wide brim which almost covered the whole of his face, but was unable to hide the grossness of the features or the cruelty of the mouth; his powerful but hunched shoulders were draped in a black cloak of ancient manufacture; his shoes had black buckles upon them. He was carrying a lantern which threw, at best, a feeble glow between himself and Lowry; this he set down and perched himself upon a wooden seat, taking something long and snaky from under his arm. He then took out a little black book and, lifting the lantern, peered intently at the pages.

"Lowry?"

"That is I."

"Huh! Frank fellow, aren't you? Well, everybody knows better than to shilly-shally with me." He spat loudly and looked back at the book. "Nice, black weather we're having, isn't it?"

"Yes. I suppose so."

"How much do you weigh, Lowry?"

"A hundred and ninety pounds."

"Hm-m-m. Hundred and ninety pounds." He found a pencil and scribbled a note in his book. Then he lifted the lantern high and took a long look at Lowry's face and body. "Hm-m-m. No deformities?"

"I don't think so."

"Hundred and ninety pounds and an ordinary neck. James Lowry, isn't it?"

"Yes."

"Well, we won't be knowing each other very long, but that's your trouble, not mine."

"What . . . what is your name?"

"Jack. It's really Jack Ketch, but you can call me Jack." He spat loudly again. "If you want to do right by me and make it easy, why just put a pound note or two in your pocket when you come up."

There was a certain odor of decay about the fellow —decay and dried blood—which made Lowry's neck hair mount. "Why a pound note?"

"Why not? I've got to eat same as you used to. I can make it pretty easy or I can make it terrible bad. Now if you want my advice, you'll just pass over a pound note or two now and we can get down to business. I hate this waiting around. It's all built there, and we'll only get mixed up more if we keep delaying things and you'll only worry about it. What do you say to that?"

"I . . . I don't know what you are talking about."

He raised the lantern and stared at Lowry. "Hm-m-m. And you look bright enough." He set the lantern back and took up the long, snaky thing from his lap. His coarse fingers became busy with it.

Lowry felt terror begin its slow seep through him. Jack Ketch. That was a familiar name. But he was certain he had never seen this man before. Jack Ketch—

Suddenly Lowry saw what the man was doing. That thing he had was a rope! And on it he was tying a hangman's noose!

And those steps. There were thirteen of them! And a platform at the top—a gallows!

"No!" screamed Lowry. "You can't do it! You have no reason to do it!"

"Hey! Hey, Lowry! Jim Lowry! Come back here! You can't run away from me! You'll never be able to run away from me! Lowry—Jim Lowry—"

The hangman's boots were thudding behind him, and the whip of the cloak was like thunder.

Lowry tried to catch himself on the brink of new steps, sensing rather than seeing them, but the steps were slippery and he could not stop. He braced himself for the shock of striking those immediately below—

But he struck nothing.

Tumbling, twisting, turning, down, down, down through an inky void with the horror of falling, a lump of agony in his stomach. Down, down, down, down, through mists and the slashing branches of trees and mists again.

And then Lowry was lying in ooze, with the feel of it squashy between his fingers and the smell of it dead and rotten. Somewhere something was moving in the blackness. Brush was crackling and something was breathing hard and hot, something searching.

As quietly as he could, Lowry crept away. It was too dark for anything to see him; if he could be silent—

"Lowry! Jim Lowry!"

Lowry pressed into the muck and lay still.

"So you don't think I can see you, Jim Lowry! Wait a moment. I have something for you."

Jack Ketch's voice was growing closer, and Lowry knew that while he could not see a thing, he must be plainly visible to Jack Ketch. Madly he leaped to his feet and floundered away; brush stung him and the half-submerged trunk of a tree tripped him and, knee-deep, he somehow kept on.

"I can tell you where you can find your hat, Jim Lowry. I want to help you." And there was a sound of spitting. "You can't get away from me."

Lowry felt warm water up as high as his knees, with ooze beneath, and the steam of it smelled decayed. He hurried through it.

"I'm trying to help you, Jim Lowry!" said Jack Ketch, seemingly closer now. "All I want to do is help you. I can tell you where to find your hat. Won't you listen to me?"

Sick and weary, Lowry fell prone and pried himself out of the mud again and floundered on.

"I don't want to hurt you," pleaded Jack Ketch's voice. "I only want to hang you!" He swore and spat. "That's what a man gets for trying to help. Lowry!

Come back here! I want to tell you where to find your hat!''

The ground was hard under his feet now, and Lowry fled swiftly through the velvet dark. A mighty force abruptly smote him on the chest and knocked him flat and half-drowned into a mauling suction of sand and sea, turning him swiftly and snatching at him and dragging him under and outward. He was drowning!

He opened his mouth to scream and choked upon the salt water; he was being held in the depths, and all around him was a greenish light, and he could see the silver bubbles of his own breath going up to the surface.

Suddenly he was on top, sucking breath into his tortured body, breath which was half sea water. He coughed and retched and tried to cry for help. And then the panic quieted in him and he found that he could stay afloat very easily. His breathing returned to normal as he treaded water and he looked anxiously for Jack Ketch, but of the hangman there was no sign. Instead there was a long, jungle strand, a yellow beach bathed in white waves, green trees of gigantic size bending over the sea. And the sky was blue and the sea was blue and there was no sound in all this peaceful serenity. Lowry thankfully dragged in the beauty of the place and wondered at the comfortable warmth which spread through him. He eyed the beach again, but not for Jack Ketch; vaguely now he remembered that he had lost something—that he had lost four hours. Somehow he had to find them despite all the warnings which he had been given; somehow he had to rearrange his memory so that he would know for certain—

The darkness was settling once more and there came a wind, at first very low and then shrill, and the waves began to stir restlessly. He was beginning to feel tired.

Suddenly he knew that there was something in the deep below which was going to strike up and snatch him down, that there were many black and awful things beyond description which would haul him under and rend him apart.

He began to swim toward the shore through the thickening dark. It took all his wits to keep from speeding in blind panic and to keep from dwelling upon the things which must be under him. There was a roaring in the air and a thunder of breaking surf, and, looking closely across the waves, he saw great towers of spume appearing and vanishing, water smashed to white frenzy on a jagged reef. He turned. He would be mashed beyond recognition if he tried to land here, and yet he knew that he could not stay long in this water, for at any moment now something would reach up and gnash him in half. But he could not turn back, for the sea seemed to be forcing him in upon the jagged black teeth which thrust up through the surf. Somewhere lightning battered blue sheets at the world. But there was no thunder beyond that of the surf. He was being raised ten feet and dropped ten feet by the surging waves, and each time he was closer to the rocks. He could not hear, he could not breathe. He was caught in a trap of water, and if he did not drown he would be smashed to a mangled mess.

Something bumped against him and he recoiled. It bumped against him a second time and he glanced toward it. A piece of wood! But even as he seized upon it he knew that it was of a peculiar design, and that he had no right to touch it.

Just above the piece of wood he sensed a presence. He looked up.

He saw a book, held by a pair of hands. That was all. Just a book and a pair of hands.

"Now hold on tight," said a somewhat oily voice. "Everything is going to be all right very soon. But you must hold on tight and close your eyes and not see anything and not hear anything but what I tell you to see and hear. Believe in me and do exactly as I tell you—"

The voice was getting faint and far away, but that was because Lowry's weary face had dropped into the soothing cushion of the water while his hands, almost nerveless, still held the piece of wood.

CHAPTER

4

It was nothing very positive, just an impression of something dark and round traveling along beside him. He jerked his head to stare at it—but there was nothing there.

Come on, now. You'll come around all right. A nice sleep in the jail will fix you up. Never did see why men had to drink— Why, it's Professor Lowry!"

The words came to him dimly, and the sensation of hands touching him at last reached his consciousness. He allowed himself to be helped from the wet pavement, feeling bruised and sore.

The rain was blowing under the street light in silver clouds which polished everything they touched; there was a damp, good smell in the night, a smell of growing and the rebirth of the soil.

Old Billy Watkins, his dark poncho streaming, was standing beside him, holding him up. Old Billy Watkins, who had been a young constable when Lowry was a kid and who had once arrested Lowry for riding a bicycle on the sidewalk and again on the complaint that Lowry had broken a window, and yet Old Billy Watkins could hold up Jim Lowry, Atworthy professor now, and be respectful if a little startled. The white mustache was damped into strings and was, for a change, washed quite clean of tobacco juice.

"I wonder," said Lowry in a thick voice, "how long I have been lying there."

"Well, now, I would put it at about five minutes or maybe six minutes. I come along here about that long ago and I got clear up to Chapel Street before I recollected that I'd forgot to put a call in at the box down here, and so I come back and here you was, lying on the sidewalk."

"What time is it?"

"Well, I guess it's pretty close to four. Sun be up

pretty soon. Is your wife sick? I see some lights on in your house."

"No. No, Billy, I guess I'm the one that's sick. I started out to take a walk—"

"Must've been unable to sleep. Now me, I find out a nice hot drink of milk is just about the thing to put a man to sleep. Are you feeling all right?"

"Yes. Yes, I guess I feel all right now."

"You must have stumbled and fell. You got a bruise on your face and you seem to have lost your hat."

"Yes . . . yes, I guess I lost my hat. I must have stumbled. What street is this?"

"Why, your street, of course. That's your house right there, not thirty feet behind you. Here, I'll help you up the steps. I heard tell you had one of them tropical diseases. Mrs. Chalmers' maid was saying it wasn't nothing bad, though. What you want to go running off into countries like that for with all them heathens, Jimmy—I mean, Professor Lowry?"

"Oh—I guess it's exciting."

"Yeah, I reckon it must be. Like my grandpap. Fighting Injuns all night and buildin' railroads all day. Now, there you are. Want me to ring the bell for you, or have you—"

"No, the door's open."

"Well, your missis took to lockin' it while you was gone and I thought maybe she still did. You look pretty pale, Ji—professor. You sure I better not call Doc Chalmers for you?"

"No, I'm all right."

"Well, by golly, you don't *look* all right. Well, maybe you know best. Good night."

"Good night, Billy."

With fascination he watched Old Billy Watkins go hobbling down the steps. But the walk was perfectly solid and Old Billy reached the street, turned back and waved and then went on up the avenue through the rain.

Lowry opened the door and went in. Water formed a pool about his feet as he took off his coat.

"Is that you, Jim?"

"Yes, Mary."

She leaned over the upper railing and then, drawing her robe about her, came swiftly down. "I've been half out of my mind. I was just about to call Tommy and have him come over so that we could look for you— Why, you're soaking wet! And you've got a bruise on your face! And what's that on your hand?"

Lowry looked down at his hand; there was another bruise there and a cut as though he had been pinched. He winced. "I fell, I guess."

"But where? You smell like . . . like seaweed."

A chill gripped him and, all concern, she threw down his coat and, regardless of the carpet, pulled him up the stairs. It was very cold in the old house and colder still in his room. She got his clothes off him and rolled him in between the covers and then wiped his face and hair with a towel.

There was a taste of salt water on his lips and a string of words sounding in his brain: "Why, the bottom is at the top, of course!"

"I should never have let you go out."

"Poor Mary. I've worried you."

"I'm not thinking about that. You're liable to be very ill because of this. Why didn't you come back when it first began to rain?"

"Mary."

"Yes, Jim?"

"I love you."

She kissed him.

"You know I'd never hurt you, Mary."

"Of course not, Jim."

"I think you're good and loyal and beautiful, Mary."

"Hush. Go to sleep."

He closed his eyes, her hand soothing upon his forehead. In a little while he slept.

He awoke to the realization that there was something horribly wrong, as if something or someone was near at hand, ready to do a thing to him. He stared around the room, but there was nothing in it; the sun was shining pleasantly upon the carpet and part of the wall, and somewhere outside people were passing and talking, and a block or two away an impatient hand was heavy upon a horn button.

It was Sunday and he ought to be thinking about going to church. He threw back the covers and stepped out of bed. His clothes were hung upon a chair, but the suit he had worn was smudged and spotted and muddy and would have to be cleaned before he could wear it again.

"Mary!"

She must be sleeping. He pulled a robe about him and went to the door of her room. She was lying with one arm flung out across the covers, her mouth parted a little and her hair forming a luminous cloud about her lovely face. She stirred and opened her eyes.

"Oh!" she said, awake. "I've overslept and we're late for church. I'll have to get breakfast and—"

"No," said Lowry. "You aren't going to church."

"But, Jim—"

"You've earned a sleep. You just lie there and be lazy, for I'm certain you haven't been in bed more than three or four hours."

"Well—"

"I'll keep up the family honor—and I'll get something to eat at the diner. You turn over and sleep—"

"My beauty sleep?"

"You don't need sleep to be beautiful." He kissed her and then, closing her door behind him, went into his room and took out a dark suit.

When he had bathed and dressed he tiptoed to her door again.

"Jim," she said sleepily, "there were some people

coming over this afternoon. I wish you'd tell them that I don't feel well or something. I don't want to go hustling about straightening up the house."

"As you will, darling."

"Tell me what the women wore," she called after him.

He was feeling almost sunny himself when he walked down the porch steps. But on the last one he halted, afraid to step to the walk. It took him some time and the feeling that he was being observed by the passers-by to make him move. But the walk was perfectly solid this morning and, again with relief and near-sunniness, he strolled to the street, nodding to people as he passed them.

The diner was nearly deserted and the blue-jowled short-order cook was having himself a cigarette and a cup of coffee at the end of the counter. He scowled when he saw someone come in and then brightened upon discovering it was Lowry.

"Well, professor! Haven't seen you since you got back."

Lowry shook Mike's soft, moist hand. "I've been pretty busy, I guess. Make it ham and eggs and coffee, Mike. And speed it up, will you? I'm late for church."

"Bell hasn't started to ring yet," said Mike, and got busy with a frying pan, grandly cracking the eggs with one hand.

"How's it feel to be back among civilized people again?" asked Mike, putting the food down before Lowry.

"I suppose so," said Lowry, not listening.

Mike, a little mystified, went back to his cup of coffee and lighted another smoke to sit broodingly, cup and cigarette both poised for use but momentarily forgotten; Mike shook his head as he gave the problem up and drank his coffee.

Lowry ate slowly, mainly because his head was a tumult of thought: Tommy's words kept passing through his mind and he could not wholly shake away the bleak forebodings Tommy had uttered, for it was unlike Tommy to jest with a man who was already worried. He had felt a gulf opening between them even as he and Tommy had talked; it was odd to seem strange and ill at ease with Tommy Williams. Why, he had even confided in Tommy that it had been he who had broken the window that time when Billy Watkins had been unable to shake the alibi; and Tommy and he had once signed a boyish pledge in blood to be friends forever.

Lowry had almost finished when he found that the food did not taste good to him; a slow feeling of quiet fear was seeping through him. Of what, he wondered, could he be afraid? The place was suddenly suffocating and he hurriedly reached for change to pay. As he placed a fifty-cent piece on the counter he caught a glimpse of the mirror between the coffee urns. There was his own face, bleak and haggard and—

Through the mirror he saw that something was behind him! A blurry, awful something that was slowly creeping upon his back!

He snapped around.

There was nothing.

He faced the mirror.

There was nothing.

"Forty cents," said Mike.

"What?"

"What'sa matter? Are you sick or something? There wasn't nothin' wrong with them eggs, was there?"

"No," said Lowry. "No. There wasn't anything wrong with the eggs."

"You forgot your change!" Mike called after him.

But Lowry was already on the sidewalk, striding swiftly away, utilizing every faculty to keep from running, to keep from glancing over his shoulder, to fight down the frozen numbness which threatened to paralyze him.

"Hello, Jim."

He dodged and then, seeing that it was Tommy, felt a surge of elation. "Hello, Tommy."

"You look shaky, old man," said Tommy. "You'd better take better care of that malaria or the old bugs will carve you hollow."

"I'm all right," said Lowry, smiling. Tommy was evidently on his way to church for he was dressed in a dark suit and a dark topcoat. Tommy, thought Jim, was a remarkably good-looking guy.

"Did you take your pills on schedule?"

"Pills?"

"Quinine or whatever you are supposed to take."

"Well—no. But I'm all right. Listen, Tommy, I don't know when I've been so glad to see anybody."

Tommy grinned. "Glad to see you, Jim."

"We've been friends for a long time," said Lowry. "How long is it now?"

"Oh, about thirty-four years. Only don't say it. When one is as old as I am and still trying to act the Beau Brummell, he doesn't like to have his age get around."

"You going to church?"

"Sure. And where else would I be going?"

"Well—" Lowry shrugged and, for some reason, chuckled.

"We've been meeting on that corner, now, at about this time, for a long while," said Tommy. "Where's Mary?"

"Oh, she didn't get much sleep last night and she's staying home today."

"I wish I had an excuse like that. Parson Bates is a baron among bores; I don't think he'd ever heard of the Old Testament until I mentioned it to him at one of his wife's endless teas."

"Tommy . . . Tommy, there's something I want to ask you."

"Fire away, old top."

"Tommy, when I left you yesterday afternoon, it was about a quarter of three, wasn't it?"

"Just about, I should imagine."

"And I did leave, didn't I?"

"Certainly, you left," replied Tommy, rather amused.

"And I only had one drink?"

"That's right. Say, this thing is really bothering you, isn't it? Don't try to hide anything from the old seer himself. What's up?"

"Tommy, I've lost four hours."

"Well! I've lost thirty-nine years."

"I mean it, Tommy. I've lost four hours and . . . and my hat."

Tommy laughed.

"It's not funny," said Lowry.

"Jim, when you look at me with those serious eyes of yours and tell me that you're half out of your mind over a hat—well, it's funny, that's all. No offense."

"I've lost four hours. I don't know what happened in them."

"Well—I suppose that would worry a fellow. But there are plenty of other hours and plenty of other hats. Forget it."

"I can't, Tommy. Ever since I lost those four hours, things have been happening to me. Terrible things." And very swiftly he sketched the events of the night just passed.

"Down the stairs," said Tommy, very sober now. "Yes. I get your point—and I get more than that."

"What's it all about?" pleaded Lowry.

Tommy walked quite a way in silence and then, seeing that they were nearing the crowd before the old church, stopped. "Jim, you won't believe me."

"I'm about ready to believe anything."

"Remember what I told you yesterday? About your article?"

"You think my article has something to do with it?"

"Yes. I believe it has. Jim, you took a very definite and even insulting stand upon a subject which has been dead for a hundred years at the very least."

"Insulting? To whom?"

"To— Well, it's hard to say, Jim, in a way that you wouldn't decry the moment it was uttered. I wouldn't try to find your hat if I were you."

"But . . . but somehow I know that if I don't find it this thing will drive me mad!"

"Steady, now. Sometimes it's even better to be mad than dead. Listen, Jim, those things you said you met— well, those are very definitely representative of supernatural forces. Oh, I know you'll object. Nobody believes in supernatural forces these days. All right. But you have met some of them. Not, of course, the real ones that might search you out—"

"You mean devils and demons?"

"That's too specific."

"Then what do you mean?"

"First Jebson. Then four hours and a hat. By the way, Jim, have you any marks on your person that you didn't have when you were with me?"

"Yes." Jim pulled up his coat sleeve.

"Hm-m-m. That's very odd. That happens to be the footprint of a hare."

"Well?"

"Oh, now, let's forget this," said Tommy. "Look, Jim. Yesterday I was feeling a little bit blue and I talked crossly about your article. Certainly, it went against the grain, for I would like to believe in the actuality of such forces—they amuse me in a world where amusement is far between. And now I am feeding these ideas of yours. Jim, believe me, if I can help you I shall. But all I can do is hinder if I put ideas into your mind. What you are suffering from is some kind of malarial kickback that doctors have not before noticed. It faded out your memory for a while and you wandered around and lost your hat. Now keep that firmly in mind. You lost your memory through malaria and you lost your hat while wandering. I'm your friend, and I'll throw everything overboard before I'll let it injure you. Do you understand me?"

"Thanks—Tommy."

"See Dr. Chalmers and have him fill you full of quinine. I'll stand by and keep an eye on you so that you won't wander off again. And I'll do that for another purpose, as well. If you see anything, then I'll see it, too. And maybe, from what I know of such things, I can keep any harm from befalling you."

"I hardly know what—"

"Don't say anything. As much as anything, I've been responsible for this with all my talk about demons and devils. I think too much of you, and I think too much of Mary to let anything happen. And—Jim."

"Yes?"

"Look, Jim. You don't think that I fed you a drug or anything in that drink?"

"No! I hadn't even thought of such a thing!"

"Well—I wondered. You know I'm your friend, don't you, Jim?"

"Yes. Of course I do. Otherwise I wouldn't run the risk of telling you these things."

Tommy walked on with him toward the church. The bell was tolling, a black shadow moving in the belfry, and the rolling circles of sound came down to surround the nicely dressed people on the steps and draw them gently in. Jim Lowry looked up at the friendly old structure; the leaves had not yet come out upon the ivy, so that great brown ropes went straggling across the gray stone; the stained glass windows gleamed in the sunlight. But somehow he felt very much out of place here. Always it seemed to him that this was a sanctuary and place of rest, but now—

A woman nudged against him in the crowd and he came to himself enough to see that it was the wife of Dean Hawkins. He remembered.

"Oh, Mrs. Hawkins!"

"Why, how do you do, Professor Lowry. Isn't your wife with you today?"

"That is what I wanted to say, Mrs. Hawkins. She is not feeling very well, and I believe she told you that she would be expecting you for tea this afternoon."

"Why, yes."

"She asked if she could beg off, Mrs. Hawkins."

"Perhaps I had better call and make sure she doesn't need something."

"No. All she needs is a little rest."

"Well, do tell her that I hope she will soon be feeling better."

"Yes, I shall," said Lowry, and then lost touch with her in the aisle.

Tommy usually sat with Lowry and Mary, and, as usual, their section of the pew was reserved for them. Lowry slid into the seat and glanced around, nodding absently to those about who nodded to him.

"She's an awful old frump," said Tommy in a whisper. "No wonder Hawkins has dyspepsia. It's a wonder she'd speak to you after the news."

"What news?" whispered Lowry, barely turning toward Tommy.

"Why, about you and Jebson. She and Mrs. Jebson are pals, and it's all over the place now. It's doubtful if she'd have called on Mary, anyway. I'm ruining my social status sitting with you. It's very funny, the way they carry on. As if you even felt bad about a fool like Jebson."

"I do feel bad. A little."

"Why? You've gotten a release from the sink of ennui. You'll be free at last from teas. You don't know when you *are* fortunate."

"What about Mary?"

"Mary has been dying to travel with you, and now you can't say 'no.' If you weren't taking it so hard, she would probably be giggling like a kid. Think of telling Mrs. Hawkins not to call! Why, can't you see it, Jim? She kicked *the* Mrs. Hawkins straight in the teeth."

"We will sing," said a distant voice, "Hymn No. 197."

The organ began to wheeze and complain, and everyone got up and dropped books and shuffled and coughed; then the nasal voice of Parson Bates cut through the scrape and din, the choir lifted tremulous wails and the service was on.

Throughout the sermon, Lowry's eyes were centered upon the back of Jebson's head; not a particularly intent gaze, but one that was broken now and then by Jebson's twisting uncomfortably. However, Lowry was barely seeing Jebson at all, but, half-lulled by Bates' dreary rhythm, was adrift out of himself, casting restively about in search of an answer.

An answer.

He knew he had to have an answer.

He knew that if he did reach an answer—

Four hours gone. And now he dimly realized that if he did not find them he was doomed, as Tommy had indirectly said, to future madness. And yet he knew instinctively and no matter how dimly, that he dared not find those four hours. No, he dared not. And yet he must!

He was on his feet again, staring blankly at the hymn book and singing more from memory than either the notes or the organ. And then he wasn't singing, but was oblivious of everything.

Some soft substance had touched against his leg.

He was afraid to look down.

He looked down.

There was nothing there.

Dry-throated and trying not to shiver, he focused his gaze upon the book and picked up the hymn. He glanced at Tommy, but Tommy was crooning along in his mellow baritone, unaware of anything at the moment but the glory of God.

The congregation was seated and a plate went the rounds while Bates read some announcements for the week. Lowry tried not to look at his feet and sought not to pull them up under the bench. He was growing more and more tense, until he did not see how he could sit there longer.

Something soft touched against his leg.

And though he had been looking straight at the spot—

There was nothing!

He clutched Tommy's sleeve, and with a muttered "Come with me," got up and started up the aisle. He knew that eyes were upon him, he knew that he dared not run, he knew that Tommy was staring at him in astonishment, but was following dutifully.

The sun was warm upon the street, and the few fresh leaves made sibilant music in the gentle wind. A kid in rags was sitting on the curb tossing a dime up and down that somebody had given him for wiping off their shoes. The chauffeur drowsed over the wheel of Jebson's car, and up the street a sleepy groom held the horses of the eccentric Mrs. Lippincott, who always came in a surrey. The horses lazily swished their tails at the few flies and now and then stamped. The headstones of the cemetery looked mellow and kind above the quiet mounds of reborn grass, and an angel spread masonry wings over "Silas Jones, R. I. P." There was the smell of fresh earth from a lawn which was being sodded, and the spice of willows from a nearby stream.

Lowry's pace slowed under the influence of the day, for he felt better now out in the open, where he could see for some distance on every side. He decided not to tell Tommy, and Tommy was asking no questions.

But as they crossed the gleaming white pavement of High Street, something flickered in the corner of Lowry's eye. It was nothing very positive, just an impression of something dark and round traveling along beside him. He jerked his head to stare at it—but there was nothing there. He glanced up to see if it could have been the shadow of a bird but, aside from some sparrows foraging in the street, there were no birds. He felt the tension begin to grow in him again.

Again he caught the faintest glimpse of it, but once more it vanished under scrutiny. And yet, as soon as he turned his head front, he could sense it once more.

Just the merest blob of darkness, very small.

A third time he tried to see it, and a third time it was gone.

"Tommy."

"Yes?"

"Look. You're going to think I'm nuts. Something touched my leg in church and there wasn't anything there. Something is coming along beside me now. I can't see it clearly, and it vanishes when I look at it. What is it?"

"I don't see anything," said Tommy, muffling his alarm. "Probably just some sun in your eye."

"Yes," said Lowry. "Yes, that's it! Just some sun in my eye."

But the merest spot of shadow, so near as he could tell, or whatever it might be, followed slowly. He increased his stride, and it came, too. He slowed in an attempt to let the thing get ahead of him, so that he could find out what it was. But it also slowed.

He could feel the tension growing.

"You'd better not say anything about this to Mary."

"I won't," promised Tommy.

"I don't want to worry her. Last night I know I did. But you won't worry her with any of this, will you?"

"Of course not," said Tommy.

"You'd better stay over at our house tonight."

"If you think you'll need me."

"I . . . I don't know," said Lowry miserably.

They walked on, and Lowry kept edging away from the thing he could almost see, so that he nearly made Tommy walk in the gutter. He was deadly afraid that it would touch him again, for he felt that if it did he would go half mad.

"Tommy."

"Yes."

"Will you walk on my right?"

"Sure."

And then Lowry could barely get an impression of it

from out of the corner of his left eye. His throat was choked as if with emery dust.

When they came to the walk before Lowry's house they paused. "No word of this to Mary," said Lowry.

"Naturally not."

"You'll stay for dinner and for the night, won't you?"

"As you will," smiled Tommy.

They went up the steps and into the hall, and at the sound of their entrance Mary came out of the living room and threw her arms about Lowry's neck and kissed him. "Well! So you've been to church, you old heathen. Hello, Tommy."

He took her extended hand. "Mary, as lovely as ever."

"Don't let the current sweetheart hear you say that," said Mary. "Staying for dinner, I hope?"

"I hope."

"Good. Now you boys go take off your coats and hats and come in here and tell me what Mrs. Hawkins looked like when I forbade her to come to tea."

"She looked awful," said Tommy. "Like she had always smelled a dead cheese in this place, anyway."

They chattered on while Lowry stood near the cold fireplace. As long as there was very deep shadow he found he could not get glimpses of the thing. That is, not at first. But when he would turn his head it would briefly seem to appear in the middle of the room. Now and then he tried to catch it napping, but each time it swiftly scuttled back. He attempted to turn his head slowly so as to lead up on it, but then, too, it kept just out of sight.

He felt that if he could only find out what it was he would feel all right about it, no matter what it was. But until he saw it— He shuddered with dread at the thought of it touching him again.

"Why, Jim!" said Mary, breaking off her conversation with Tommy. "You're shivering again." She put her hand upon his arm and led him toward the door. "Now you go right upstairs and take ten grains of quinine and then lie down for a little nap. Tommy will help me put the dinner on and keep me company, won't you, Tommy?"

"Anything for a friend," said Tommy.

It made Jim vaguely uneasy to leave them together. But, then, Tommy must have been here many times while he was gone in just as innocent a capacity. What was wrong with him? To think that way about Tommy! About his best and really only friend? He started up the stairs.

And step by step the "thing" jumped along with him. He pressed himself against the wall to avoid any possibility of contact with it, but the presence of the wall, barring any dodge he might make, made him feel even more nervous.

What was the thing, anyhow?

Why was it tagging him?

What would it do to him?

What would make it go away?

He shivered again.

In his room he found his quinine and, taking it to the bath to get a glass of water, was accompanied by the "thing." He could see it very indistinctly against the white tile. And then he grew cunning. He guided it by slowly turning his head, and then, springing sideways and out the door, he banged the door behind him. He felt better as he downed the quinine and water. For a moment he had the inane notion that he ought to go and tell Mary not to open this door, but then, of course, it would be a much better idea to lock it. He found a key in a bedroom door and carried it to the bath. In a moment the lock clicked home. He almost laughed aloud, and then caught himself up. That wouldn't do. Whatever the thing was, it was perfectly explainable. Something wrong with his eyes, that was all. It was just malaria. Something the doctors hadn't discovered about it.

He went to his bedroom and took off his jacket and stretched out on his bed. The warm air from the open window was very soothing, and in a little while he drifted off into a quiet sleep, untroubled by dreams.

Some three hours later he roused himself. The sun was shining upon his face and he felt too warm. Downstairs he heard Mary calling to him that dinner was ready. Wasn't dinner a little late for Sunday? It must be nearly four, according to the sun.

He got up, yawning and stretching and feeling much better for his rest; he felt good about something he had done, but he could not quite remember, in his half-awake state, just what it was.

The pleasant sound of very high, musical laughter

came to him, and for a moment he thought it was Mary. But then he knew that it could not be, for Mary had a low, husky laugh that made him feel warm and comfortable inside, and this laugh—there was something unearthly about it. Hadn't he heard it before?

He leaped up and opened the hall door, but it was not coming from downstairs. He went to the window and looked out, but there wasn't anyone on the walk or in the yard. Where was the laughter coming from? What was it that was laughing?

And then he saw a movement as though something had run down the wall to get behind him. He whirled. There was a flurry as if something had dived behind him again. He spun around.

But it was to no avail. And the thing he had so carefully locked away was still with him—and the thing was the source of the laughter.

What a mad laugh it was!

He felt very tired. Best to ignore it, whatever it was; best to walk around and not hear and not see it; best to pretend that it wasn't there at all. Would Mary and Tommy hear it?

Resignedly he went to the bathroom and washed.

"Jim? Jim, you old ox, aren't you ever coming down?"

"Coming, Mary." He'd better not appear too shaken.

When he entered the dining room the table was

spread with bright crystal and silver and china, and a big capon was steaming away on a platter flanked by mashed potatoes and green peas.

"Well, sir! You look better," said Tommy.

"He didn't get any sleep last night," said Mary. "Come, Jim, m'lad, up with the tools and carve away."

He sat down at the head of the board, and Tommy sat at his right. He looked down the table at Mary and smiled. How beautiful was this wife of his, and how tingly she made him feel when she looked at him that way. To think he would wonder about whether she loved him or not! No woman could look at a man that way unless she truly loved him.

He picked up the knife and carving fork and started to pin down the capon. Then, suddenly, the knife was shaking so that he could not hold it. There was a clatter as it fell against china.

Just a shrill, musical laugh right behind him!

"Tommy," he said, trying to speak distinctly, "Tommy, would you mind doing the honors? I guess I'm pretty shaky."

Mary was instantly concerned, but somehow Jim passed it off. Tommy went to work on the capon and Mary served up the vegetables—stealing quiet glances of wonder at Jim. Then everything was all served and they were ready to begin.

"Some chicken," said Tommy.

"Ought to be, what it cost!" said Mary. "The price of food can't go any higher and still let the clouds go by."

"Yeah," said Tommy in a slow drawl, "and wages

stay the same. That is what is known as economic progress—get everything so high that nobody can buy so that there will be a surplus which the government can buy and throw away so that the taxpayer will have less money with which to buy higher-priced goods. Yes, we've certainly improved civilization since the days when we lived in caves."

Mary laughed and, shockingly, the thing laughed, too, behind Jim. But it was an accidental combining, for a moment later, at a serious statement from Tommy, it laughed again.

Jim had picked up knife and fork two or three times. But another strange thing was occurring. Each time he started to touch his plate it moved. Not very much, just a little. A sort of easy, circular motion which ceased as soon as he did not choose to touch it again; but when he did, it did. Very carefully he found cause to help himself to more gravy, and then, swiftly, glanced under the cloth and the pad. But there was nothing wrong. He put back the plate and once more addressed himself to it. Once more it moved.

He felt ill.

"Would . . . would you two please excuse me? I . . . I guess I don't feel very well."

"Jim!"

"Better let me send for a doctor," said Tommy. "You look very white."

"No. No, I'm all right. Just let me lie down for a little while."

"I'll keep your dinner warm," said Mary.

"It was such a good dinner, too," said Lowry with a sad grin. "Don't worry about me. Just go ahead."

And then the laughter sounded again, higher and shriller, and the dark shadow scuttled along beside him as he hurried through the door and back to his bed. He flung himself down. And then, thinking better of it, he leaped up and shot home the bolt. Again he lay down, but he found he did not have sufficient control over himself. Tight-throated and half sick, he began to pace a narrow circle around his room.

CHAPTER

5

There was a gentle purring sound, and the dark object loomed higher. Something began slowly to pry Lowry's fingers off the ledge.

A clock downstairs struck eleven in long, slow strokes. Lowry, face down upon his bed, stirred uneasily and came up through the kindly oblivion of a doze. He woke to the realization that something horrible was about to happen to him, but, lying for a while in stupor, pushing back the frontiers of his consciousness, he picked up memory after memory, inspected it and cast it aside. No, no one of these things had any bearing on his present condition, there was nothing that he knew about which might have caused—

A shrill tinkle of laughter reached him.

He came up quivering in every muscle and saw the thing scurry around the bottom of his bed and get out of sight. If only he could get a full glimpse of it!

There was paper rattling somewhere, stirred by the warm night breeze, as though something in the room was sorting out his letters. And though the room seemed empty to him, after a little a single sheet, drifting on the air, came fluttering down to the carpet by his feet. He stared at it, afraid to pick it up. He could see writing upon it. Finally his curiosity overcame his fear, and he opened it and tried to read. But it was written in some ancient, incomprehensible script that blurred and ran together. The only thing legible was a time, and he could not even be sure of that.

"... 11:30 to ... "

He peered into the shadows of the room, but aside from what had dived under his bed, he was apparently alone. Had this thing come floating in with the wind?

Eleven thirty? Was this a bid for an appointment

somewhere? Tonight? He shuddered at the thought of going forth again. But, still, wasn't it possible that he might have a friend somewhere who was volunteering to help him find his four hours? And tonight he would be wary and step down no steps which he did not know had something solid at the bottom.

He got up, and instantly the little dark thing got behind him, permitting him only the slightest of glimpses. Within him he could feel a new sensation rising, a nervous anger of the kind men feel in remembering times when they have shown cowardice.

For he knew very clearly that he was being a coward. He was letting these things drag the reason out of his mind without even offering to combat them; he was being thrust about like a scarecrow in a hurricane, and the things were laughing at him, perhaps even pitying him! His fists clenched into hard hammers; God knows he had never been found lacking in courage before, why should he cower like a sniveling cur and allow all things to steamroller him? His jaws were tight, and he felt his heart lunging inside him, and he ached to join in wild battle and put down forever the forces which were seeking to destroy him.

He took a topcoat from the closet and slipped into it. From a drawer he drew a Colt .38 and pocketed it. Into his other pocket he put a flashlight. He was through being a coward about this. He would meet his ghosts and batter them down.

Eleven thirty? Certainly something would lead him

to the rendezvous. Perhaps something was waiting for him out in the street now.

The high laughter tinkled again, and he spun around and sought to kick the dark object, but again it eluded him. Never mind—he would deal with that later.

Quietly he slipped out of his room. Mary's light was off, and her door was closed. There was no use disturbing her. Tommy must be in the guest room at the head of the stairs, for the door there was slightly ajar. Masking the flashlight with his fingers so that a small segment of its light played upon the bed, he looked at Tommy. Without his cynically twisted grin, Tommy was really a very beautiful fellow, thought Lowry. And Tommy, in sleep, looked as innocent as a choir boy. Lowry crept down the stairs and out the front door, to stand in the shadow of the porch and stare at the walk.

It was warm tonight, and what little breeze there was whispered faintly and sweetly across the lawns. The moon was nearly full and rode in a clear sky, from which it had jealously blotted the smaller stars.

Lowry went down the middle of the steps and dared the walk to open up. It did not. Almost smiling over this small triumph, he reached the street and cast about him. Eleven thirty was not here, but he was almost certain that if he was expected there would be a guide.

The little dark thing flicked about his legs, and the

laughter sounded, gently as a child's. Lowry nerved himself to listen to it.

Tonight he would not cower and run away. These things had been strange to him before, but they were not strange to him now. Something would come to lead him, and he would be brave and carry out—

"Jim!"

He saw Tommy silhouetted in an upstairs window.

"Jim! Where are you going?"

But there was something moving under a tree ahead and it was beckoning to him.

"Jim! At least wait until I give you your hat!"

He felt a cold shudder race over him. The thing was beckoning more strenuously, and he sped toward it.

At first he could not make out what it was, so deep was the moon shadow there. But in a moment he saw that it was a cassocked little figure not more than four feet high, with a nearly luminous bald head. Beads and a cross hung about its neck, and crude leather sandals exposed its toes.

"You received my message?"

"Yes. Where are we going?" asked Lowry.

"You know as well as I do, don't you?"

"No."

"Well-l-l-l— You know me, don't you?"

Lowry looked at him more closely. There seemed to be an intangible quality to this little monk, as if he was lacking substance. And then Lowry found that he could see through him and behold the tree trunk and the moon-bathed curb.

"I am Sebastian. You turned me out of my tomb about six years ago. Don't you remember?"

"The church tombs of Chezetol!"

"Ah, you do remember. But do not think I am angry. I am a very humble fellow, and I am never angry, and if I have to wander now without a home, and if my body was the dust which your diggers' spades broke, I still am not angry. I am a very humble person." And, indeed, he was almost cringing. But still there was a certain sly way he cast his eyes sideways at Jim that made one wonder. "I had been lying there for three hundred years, and you, thinking it was an old Aztec ruin because of the Aztec symbols on the stones which had been converted to its construction, dug me up. Where is my belt?"

"Your belt?"

"Yes, my beautiful golden belt. You picked it up and turned to your guide and said, 'What's this? A gold belt marked with the symbols of the Catholic Church! I thought this was an Aztec ruin. A week's digging for nothing but a golden belt.'"

"It is in the college museum."

"I was a little hurt about it," said Sebastian sadly. "'—for nothing but a golden belt.' I liked it because I made it, you see, and we thought it was very beautiful. We converted Razchytl to Christianity, and then we took his gold and made sacred vessels of it, and when he died on the mining gangs we even went so far as to bury him with a golden cross. May I have my belt?"

"I can't get it for you now."

"Oh, yes, you must. Otherwise I won't go with you and show you."

"Show me what?"

"Where you spent your four hours."

Lowry pondered for a little while and then nodded. "All right. We'll get your belt. Come with me."

Lowry walked swiftly up the street, the little dark shadow just behind the range of his eye to the left, Sebastian a step behind upon his right. Sebastian's crude slippers made no sound upon the pavement.

It was a very short distance to the building which housed the museum, and Lowry was soon fumbling for his keys. The door opened into the blackness, but Lowry knew the place by heart and did not turn on his light until he was near the case which held the golden belt. He fumbled for more keys and, switching on his flash, started to fit one. He stopped. He played his light upon the objects within. The belt was gone!

Nervously he turned to Sebastian. "The belt isn't here. They must have sold it to another museum while I was gone."

Sebastian's head was cast down. "It is gone, then. And I shall never get it back—but I am not angry. I am a very humble person. I am never angry. Good-by, Señor Lowry."

"Wait! I'll try to get your belt back! I'll buy it back and put it somewhere where you can find it!"

Sebastian paused at the door and then dodged aside. A beam of light stabbed down the aisle. It was Terence, the college watchman.

"Who is in here?" cried Terence, trying to make his voice sound very brave.

"It is I," said Lowry, moving into the path of the light and blinking at its source.

"Oh. Professor Lowry! Sure, and you gave me an awful scare there for a moment. This is no time to be tinkering around with them trinkets."

"I was doing some research," said Lowry. "I needed a certain inscription for a class lecture tomorrow."

"Did you find it?"

"No. It isn't here any more. I suppose they've sold it."

"Jebson would sell his own mother, Professor Lowry, and I mean what I say. He's cut my pay, that's what he's done. I was terribly sorry to hear what he did to you. I thought that was a pretty good article you wrote, too."

"Thank you," said Lowry, moving to the door, panicky lest Sebastian be frightened away.

"Course you laid it on a bit thick, Professor Lowry. Now, in the old country I could show you people that could tell you about having met a lot of things they couldn't explain. It ain't healthy to go around begging the demons to smash you."

"Yes. Yes, I'm sure it isn't. I've got to be going, Terence, but if you'd like to drop around to my office some afternoon when you get up, I'd be glad to hear about your evidence."

"Thank you, Professor Lowry. Thank you. That I will."

"Good night, Terence."

"Good night, Professor Lowry."

Lowry walked swiftly toward the deepest shade of the street, and when he was sure he was out of Terence's sight he began to cast around for some sign of Sebastian. But all he could glimpse was the occasional flick of the dark object which traveled with him.

When he had searched around and about for nearly twenty minutes, a low call reached him. And there was Sebastian hiding by a bush.

"Oh," said Lowry in relief. "I hoped you hadn't gone. I wanted to tell you that if you would wait awhile I would buy back the golden belt."

"I am not angry," said Sebastian.

"But you want your belt, don't you?"

"It would please me very much. It was such a pretty belt. I made it with my own hands with many humble prayers to God, and though the metal is heathen the work was the work of love."

"You shall have your belt. But tonight you must take me to the place where I can find the four hours."

"You are determined to find them, then?"

"I am."

"Jim Lowry, I wonder if you know what it will cost to find them."

"Whatever the cost, I intend to do so."

"You are brave tonight."

"Not brave. I know what I must do, that is all."

"Jim Lowry, last night you met some things."

"Yes."

"Those things were all working on your side. They were the forces of good. You did not lose your four hours to them, Jim Lowry. Nor to me."

"I must find them."

"You could not conceive the forces of the other side. You could not conceive so much pain and terror and evil. If you are to find those four hours you must be prepared to face those other forces."

"I must find them."

"Then, Jim Lowry, have faith in me and I shall show you part of the way. The rest of the way you must go alone."

"Lead and I shall follow."

Sebastian's delicate little hand made the sign of the cross upon the air and then moved out to point an upward way. Lowry found that he was upon a smoothly blue roadway which wound upward and onward as though to the moon itself.

Sebastian gripped his beads and began to walk. Lowry glanced around him, but for all he searched, he could not find the small black object, nor could he hear its laughter—if it was the source of that laughter.

They went a long way, past spreading fields and little

clusters of sleeping houses. Once a thing with bowed head and hidden face passed them, going down with slow and weary steps, but Lowry could not understand what it was.

The way began to be broken as though it had once consisted of steps which had disintegrated to rubble; tufts of grass began to be more frequent in the cracks, showing that the way was little used. Ahead, a smoky outline of mountains took slow form and then it seemed to Lowry that they had come upon them swiftly. The road began to writhe and dip on hillsides, lurching out and then standing almost on edge toward the inside, as though earthquakes and avalanches had here been steadily at work. And even as they passed over it, it occasionally trembled, and once, with a sigh which ended in a roar, a whole section of it went out behind them, leaving a void. Lowry began to worry about ever being able to get back.

"It gets more difficult now," said Sebastian. "Have you ever climbed mountains?"

"Not often."

"Well—you look strong enough."

Sebastian headed off at right angles to the dwindling road and walked easily up a nearly vertical cliff. Lowry reached up and found to his astonishment that although the cliff had looked very high at first, it was only eight or nine feet and he ascended easily. For a way, then, they walked along its rim, and the road fell swiftly away until it was less than a white string. The wind was a little stronger up here, but it was still warm, and the moon was friendly. There seemed to be good cause for them to be as unseen as possible, for now Sebastian was pressing back against yet another cliff, one which really was high.

"It is a little worse now," said Sebastian. "Be very careful."

They had come to the end of both cliffs, and here a right-angle turn folded away from them, offering only rough stone to their questing touch.

Lowry looked down and felt slightly ill. He disliked height no more than another man, but the cliff here pitched off forever and was consecutive in his sight, so that he could visualize falling through that space. Far, far down a small stream, like a piece of bright wire, wound its way through a rocky gorge, and here and there on the vertical face, trees, diminutive with distance, jutted out like staying hands. Sebastian had gone on around the turn. Lowry reached, and then reached again, but he could find no purchase.

Leaning far out, he saw a ledge. It seemed to him that if he could half fall and reach at the same time, he could grip it. He leaned out, he snatched wildly. He had hold of the ledge, and his legs were being pulled at by the drop below.

"Work along," said Sebastian.

Lowry inched himself along. It was very hard to keep hold of the ledge, for it was rough and hurt his hands and sloped a trifle outward. He tried to see Sebastian, but he could not because of his own arm. He began to be weary, and a nausea of terror came into him, as though something was staring at him, ready to pry him loose. He stared up at the ledge.

A great splotch of black was hovering there, and two large eyes peered luminously down with malevolence!

Lowry glanced down and saw emptiness under him.

There was a gentle, purring sound, and the dark object loomed higher. Something began slowly to pry Lowry's fingers off the ledge.

"Sebastian!"

There was no answer from the monk.

"Sebastian!"

The purring over his head grew louder and more pleased.

One hand was almost loose, and then it was loose! Lowry dangled in space as the thing began slowly and contentedly to loosen his left hand. He remembered the gun and snatched it from his pocket and pointed it up.

The eyes did not change. The purring was softer. Suddenly Lowry was aware of a reason he could not pronounce that he must not shoot. To do so would bring a whole pack down upon him, and it was doubtful if his bullets would take any effect. His left hand came free and he swooped away from the ledge with the air screaming past his face and up his nose, and the greedy dark drowning him.

He was aware of stars and the moon all mingled in

a spinning dance, and the cliff side rolling upward at incredible speed, and the bright wire of the stream but little closer than it had been when he had first begun to fall.

He had no memory of landing. He was lying on a surface so smooth that it was nearly metallic. Stunned, he got to his knees and stared over the edge of this second ledge, to find that the stream was still down there, but that his fall had evidently been broken by trees.

Where was Sebastian?

He looked up but could find no sign of the thing which had pried him loose. He looked to the right and left, but he could discover no descent from this place. Pressing against the cliff, he edged along. There were small caves here whose dark mouths held things he could sense but dimly. He knew he must not enter them. But still—still, how else could he ever get down?

One cave was larger than the rest, and though his resolution had ebbed considerably, he knew that he must go in. On hands and knees he crept over the lip, and his hands met a furry something which made him leap back. Something struck him lightly from behind and drove him to his knees once more. The floor of this place was furry, all of it, dry and ticklish to the touch.

A deep, unconcerned voice said, "Go along ahead of me, please."

He dared not look back at the speaker, whatever it was. He got up and went along. There were great flat ledges in the place over which he stumbled now and then. Evidently he had lost his flashlight, but he would have been afraid to have used it. There was something awful in this place, something he could not define, but which waited in patient stillness for him perhaps around the next bend, perhaps around the one after that— He came up against a rough wall which bruised him.

"Please go along," said the voice behind him in a bored fashion.

"Where . . . where is Sebastian?" he ventured.

"You are not with *them* now. You are with us. Be as little trouble as you can, for we have a surprise waiting for you down one of these tunnels. The opening, you poor fool, is on your right. Don't you remember?"

"I . . . I've never been here before?"

"Oh, yes, you have. Oh, yes, indeed, you have. Hasn't he?"

"Certainly he has," said another voice at hand.

"Many, many times."

"Oh, not many," said the other voice. "About three times is all. That is, right here in this place."

"Go along," yawned the first voice.

It was all he could do to force his legs to work. Something unutterably horrible was waiting for him, something he dared not approach, something which, if he saw it, would drive him mad!

"You belong to us now, so go right along."

"What are you going to do with me?"

"You'll find out."

There was an incline under his feet, and at each step things seemed to wake beneath his feet and go slithering away, nearly tripping him, sometimes curling about his ankles, sometimes striking hard against him.

The incline was very long, and there was blackness at its bottom. He must not go down here! He must not go down here! He had to turn back while there was yet time!

"Go along," said the bored voices. "You are ours now."

Ahead there was only stillness. Ahead— Lowry sank down on the rump, too ill and weak to go on, too terrified of what lay just ahead to take another step. Everything was spinning and things were howling at him.

And then he heard Sebastian's quiet little voice speaking long, monotonous sentences in Latin.

Sebastian!

Lowry pulled himself up and staggered on toward the sound. He was not sure but what the way had forked and that he had taken another route down. He was not sure of anything but Sebastian's voice.

He rounded a corner and blinked in a subdued light which came from a stained window high up. This place was mainly shadows and dust, but little by little he made out other things. There were seven bulls, carved from stone, all along a high ledge; and each bull had one hoof poised upon a round ball as his incurious stone eyes regarded the scene below.

The floor was very slippery, so that it was hard to stand, and Lowry hung hard upon a filthy drapery on his right.

The room was full of people, half of them men, half of them women, with Sebastian standing at a tiny altar a little above their heads. Sebastian's graceful hands were making slow, artistic motions over the heads, and his eyes were raised upward to meet the rays which came down from the high window. A gigantic book was open before him, and a cross and sacred ring lay upon it to hold its place. And around him, in a wide circle, filed the women.

They were lovely women, all dressed in white save for the single flash of red which came from their capes as they moved; their faces were saintly and innocent, and their movements graceful and slow.

Just outside this moving circle of women stood another circle, but of men. These were also dressed in white, but their faces were not pure; rather, they were grinning and evil. Their white capes were stained with something dark which they made no effort to hide.

Sebastian prayed on and moved his hands over their heads to bless them. The circle of women moved slowly and quietly around him, but did not look up at him save when they passed the front of the altar. The circle of men paid no attention whatever to Sebastian.

And then Lowry was made almost to cry out. For he saw what they were doing. As the circle of women passed behind the altar, the men would suddenly reach out with clawed hands, and the women, with abruptly lascivious eyes, would glance over the shoulder at the men, and then, with re-formed innocence of expression, file past the front of the altar again. The men would jostle and snicker

118

to one another, and then the next time reach out again.

Sebastian prayed on, his tender eyes upon the square of light.

Lowry tried to get away, but the floor was so slippery he could hardly stand and could not run. And then he saw what made the floor so slippery. It was an inch thick in blood!

He screamed.

Everyone whirled to stare at him. Sebastian stopped praying and bent a kindly smile upon him. All the rest muttered among themselves and pointed and scowled, an undertone of anger growing from them.

The seven bulls upon the ledge came to life with a bellow. They moved their hoofs and the balls rolled, and it could be seen then that they had had human skulls there. Again they moved their hoofs, and the skulls came tumbling down from the ledge to strike in the midst of the angry mob, felling some of the women and men, but not touching Sebastian.

Lowry could not run. He could not breathe. The mob was howling with rage now, and evidently thinking he had thrown the skulls, surged forward toward him.

Just before they reached him he was able to make the incline. As swiftly as he could he raced up it. A sinuous shape shot out and barred his way.

"Where are you going?"

Madly Lowry ripped it away and raced on.

A blow from behind felled him and a voice cried, "Where are you going? You must stay here and see it through!" But Lowry got to his feet and dashed away. He could hear the roar of the mob fading, but he knew that there were other things around him now, flying just above and behind him, striving to dive down and cut off his retreat.

He crashed into a wall, and then when he rose up and strove to find a way out, there was none. The roar of the mob was growing louder. He tore his hands as he tried to find the exit. Then there were knives flashing, and the cold bite of one against his wrist was instantly warmed by the flow of his own blood. He pitched forward and fell from a height. There was grass in his fingers and moonlight above him, and he leaped up and raced away, running through sand which reduced his speed and made him stumble. He could still hear whirring sounds above and behind him. He was outdistancing the mob, but could he never get free of those shapes?

"Sebastian!"

But there was no Sebastian.

"Sebastian!"

And just the whir of the things overhead and the blurred glimpses of things that raced with him. The moon was white upon a wide expanse, not unlike a dried-up lake of salt. He was out in the open now, and there was neither hiding place nor refuge. He was out in the open and being hunted by things he could not see, things which wanted to take him back!

A shadowy shape loomed ahead, still afar. He forced himself to slow down and turn off away from it. There was something about its hat, something about the dark cloak, something about the thing which dangled from its hand—

Jack Ketch!

There was a ravine, and he scrambled down it. He crept along its bottom and went deep into a shadowy grove which he found there. Something was calling to him now, but he could not tell what the words were. Something calling which must never, never find him here! There were white mountains around him and high above him, and they offered refuge to him and he went deeper into them.

The trees were thicker and the grass was soft and protective.

Something was beating through the bushes in an attempt to locate him, and he lay very still, pressing hard against the earth. The something came nearer and nearer, and the voice was muttering.

And then the voice receded and the crackling sounds grew fainter and Lowry stretched out at length in the dewy grass, getting his breath. The moonlight made delicate shadow patterns about this place, and the night wind was warm and caressing. He began to breathe quietly, and the hammering of his heart lessened.

It was an almost triumphant feeling which went through him then. He had not found his lost four hours!

He had not found them! He raised himself a trifle and cupped his chin in his hands, staring unseeingly at the white thing just before him.

He had not found his four hours!

And then his eyes focused upon the thing before which he lay. He was conscious that he was lying half across a mound, and that there was the fresh smell of flowers too late growing for spring.

There was writing upon that white stone.

But what kind of writing?

He inched a little closer and read:

JAMES LOWRY
Born 1901
Died 1940
Rest In Peace

He recoiled.

He got to his knees and then to his feet. The whole night was spinning and the high, shrill laughter was sounding again and the little dark shape dashed around to get out of his sight.

With a piercing cry he spun about and raced madly away.

He had found peace for a moment, peace and rest, before the headstone of his own future grave!

CHAPTER

6

. . . obviously he had lost a great deal of weight, for his cheeks were sunken, and a pallor as gray as the belly of a rain cloud gave him a shock, so much did it cause him to resemble a dead man.

When he awoke the following morning he knew by the position of the sun on the wall that he still had at least half an hour before he had to rise. Usually, when that was the case, he could lie and stretch and inch down in the covers and relish his laziness. But there was something different about this morning.

A robin was sitting in a tree outside his window, cocking its head first to one side and then to another as it sought to spy worms from that ambitious altitude; now and then the bird would forget about worms and loose a few notes of joyous exuberance, to have them answered from another part of the yard. Somewhere, early as it was, a lawn mower was running, and its peculiarly cheerful whir was augmented by a careless, tuneless whistle. Somewhere a back door slammed and a pup yipped for a moment, and then evidently saw another dog and began a furious fanfare of ferocious warning. Downstairs, Lowry could hear Mary singing in an absentminded way, going no more than half a chorus to a song he could not quite recognize. On the second-floor hall, just outside his door, he heard a board creak; somehow there was menace in the sound.

The knob of the door turned soundlessly and a minute crack appeared; another board creaked and a hinge protested in a hushed tone. Lowry half closed his eyes, pretending to be asleep, and saw the door come open a trifle more. He became rigid.

Tommy's face, crowned by disheveled dark hair, was just beyond the opening, and Tommy's hand upon the knob glittered with its class ring. Lowry lay still.

Evidently Tommy was satisfied that Lowry slept, for he crossed the threshold with soundless tread and moved to the foot of the bed. For a little while Tommy stood there, looking out from an immobile face, as though ready to smile and say good morning in case Lowry awoke—and if he did not, then—

Lowry's eyes were very nearly shut, enough to deceive an observer but not enough to blank out Tommy. Why, Lowry asked himself, did he lie here faking like this? What strangeness was there about Tommy which bade such a precaution?

The robin evidently spotted a worm, for he let out a call and dived out of sight toward the lawn. A housewife was calling after a little boy and adding to a hasty grocery order.

Tommy stayed where he was, studying Lowry, until he seemed quite sure that Lowry still slept, and then, with a glance toward the door as though to make sure that Mary was still downstairs, he came silently up along the side of the bed.

It was Lowry's impulse to reach up and snatch at Tommy's white shirt, but some latent protective sense combined with his curiosity to let matters take their course. Tommy's hand moved gracefully across Lowry's eyes—once, and then twice. A numb sensation began to creep over Lowry.

Now was the time to move. He would awake and greet Tommy— But he couldn't move. He seemed to be frozen. And Tommy leaned over until their faces were not three inches apart. For an instant Lowry thought he saw fangs in Tommy's mouth, but before he could gain a whole impression the teeth had again foreshortened.

Tommy stayed there for more than a minute and then straightened up, a cold smile taking the beauty from his face. He passed his hand again across Lowry's forehead and, with a quiet nod, turned and stole out into the hall. The door clicked slowly shut behind him.

It was some time before Lowry could move, and when he did he was weak. He sat on the edge of the bed, feeling shaky, as a man might who has just given a blood transfusion. When he had assembled enough energy he approached the mirror and, gripping the bureau top with both hands, stared at himself.

His eyes were so far sunken in his head beneath his shaggy brows that he could barely make out his own pupils; his hair was matted; his face seemed to have lost a certain pugnacity with which he had always attempted to compensate for his shyness; obviously he had lost a great deal of weight, for his cheeks were sunken, and a pallor as gray as the belly of a rain cloud gave him a shock, so much did it cause him to resemble a dead man.

He forgot the cost of his exertions and swiftly tried to wipe out the ravages of nerve strain by carefully shaving and bathing and grooming, and when he again looked into the mirror, tying his cravat, he was a little heartened.

After all, here it was a fresh spring day. Devil take

Jebson; the old fool would be dead long before James Lowry. Devil take the four hours; as the knight had said, what were four hours? Devil take the phantoms which had assailed him. He had courage enough and strength enough to last them out. He had too much courage and will power to cause him to back down upon his original assertions in the article. Let them do their worst!

He trotted down the steps, buttoning his jacket, holding up his spirits with an effort which resembled the use of physical strength. The dark thing was just beside and behind him, and the high, shrill laughter sounded in the distance, but he was determined not to give them the satisfaction of heed. Despite them, he would carry on and act as he had always acted. He would greet Mary and Tommy with pleasantness, and he would lecture his class as dryly and lengthily as ever.

Mary looked him askance at first, and then, seeing that he was apparently much better, threw her arms about his neck and gave him her cheery good-morning kiss. Tommy was already seated at the table.

"See?" said Mary. "You can't hurt the old block of granite. He's chipper as ever."

"Darned if you aren't," said Tommy. "By the way, Jim, eleven thirty at night isn't exactly the time for a stroll. Hope you kept out of trouble."

He felt a momentary resentment toward Tommy for mentioning it. It was as though Tommy himself wished to keep these hateful events before his eyes. But then Tommy was asking in a very friendly way which could involve no harm. Still—that strange visit, and—

"Here's your breakfast," said Mary, setting a plate of ham and eggs before him. "You don't have to hurry, but I'd advise you to start now."

Lowry smiled at her and seated himself at the head of the board. He took up his knife and fork, still thinking about Tommy. He started to take a bite of eggs—

Ever so gently, the plate moved.

Lowry glanced to see if Tommy or Mary had noticed. Evidently they hadn't. Again he started to take a mouthful of eggs.

Again the plate went slightly from side to side.

He laid down his fork.

"What's the matter?" said Mary.

"I . . . I guess I'm not very hungry."

"But you haven't eaten anything since breakfast yesterday!"

"Well—" Bravely he took up his fork. Slowly the plate moved. And as he stared at it he was aware of something else.

When he was not looking at Tommy he could see from the corner of his eyes that Tommy seemed to have fangs. He stared straight at the man, but there was nothing extraordinary about Tommy's mouth. He must be imagining things, thought Lowry. He again bent over his plate.

But there could be no doubt about the validity of that impression. The second he took his eyes from Tommy's face, Tommy possessed yellow fangs which depressed the outside of his lower lip!

The plate moved.

The little dark thing scuttled behind him.

Somewhere the high shrill laughter sounded.

With all his courage exerted, Lowry managed to sit still. He looked at his plate. As long as he did not try to touch it, it was perfectly quiet.

Then he saw something else. When he took his eyes away from Mary, *she* seemed to have fangs not unlike Tommy's!

He stared at her, but her face was its own sweet self.

He looked away.

Mary's mouth was marred by those yellow fangs!

If he could only see their mouths looking straight at them! Then he could be sure!

The dark thing scuttled out of sight.

He tried to eat and the plate moved.

He sprang back from the table, upsetting his chair. Mary looked at him with frightened eyes. Tommy, too, got up.

"I've got to see somebody before my first class," said Lowry in a carefully schooled voice.

He looked at Tommy and saw Mary's fangs. He looked at Mary and she was herself, but he could see Tommy's fangs.

Hurriedly he went out into the hall and snatched up his topcoat, aware that Tommy had followed him and was getting into his. Mary stood before him and looked wonderingly up into his face.

"Jim, is there something I should know about? You can trust us, Jim."

He kissed her and seemed to feel the fangs he could not wholly see. "I'm all right, dear. Don't worry about me. There's nothing wrong."

She plainly did not believe him, and she was thinking furiously, for it was not until he was at the bottom of the steps—and glad to find the walk solid—that she called, "Your hat, Jim!"

He waved at her and strode out to the street. Tommy found it difficult keeping up with him.

"Jim, old boy, what's the matter with you?"

When he wasn't looking at Tommy he could see those fangs very clearly—and a sly, meaningful look on Tommy's face. "There's nothing the matter."

"But there is, Jim. You leave the table last night and then, at eleven or eleven thirty, or whatever it was, you go chasing forth as though possessed by a thousand devils, and now you fling away from the table. There's something you aren't telling me, Jim."

"You know the answer," said Jim sullenly.

"I . . . I don't get you."

"You were the one that started telling me about demons and devils."

"Jim," said Tommy, "you think I have something to do with what is happening to you?"

"I'm almost sure of it."

"I'm glad you said 'almost,' Jim."

"There was that drink, and then everything went black for four hours and I lost—"

"Jim, there's no poison or anything in the world that could cause such a blankness and leave no effect. Grant me that, Jim."

"Well—"

"And you know it," said Tommy. "Whatever is happening to you has nothing whatever to do with me."

"Well—"

"Let's not quarrel, Jim. I only want to help you."

Jim Lowry was silent, and they walked on in silence. Lowry was hungry now, and ahead the diner was full of clamor and the smell of coffee. He tried not to remember what had happened to him here yesterday.

"You go on," said Jim to Tommy. "I've got to see somebody in there."

"As you say, Jim. Will I see you at lunch?"

"I suppose so."

Tommy nodded to him and strode away. Lowry went in and perched himself on a stool.

"Well!" said Mike, relieved that he had not lost a customer through his garrulousness. "What'll it be, sir?"

"Ham and eggs," said Jim Lowry.

He was relieved to find that this plate did not move. And it began to be born in him that Tommy must have quite a bit to do with what was happening to him. He ate like a starved man.

Half an hour later he entered his classroom. It was good to be in such a familiar place, good to stand up here on the platform and watch the students pass the door in the hall. Presently they would come in here and he would begin to drone along on the subject of ancient beliefs in ancient civilizations and perhaps, after all, everything was right with the world.

He glanced around to see if everything was in place, if the board was clean for his notes—

He stared at the board behind the platform. That was strange. These were always washed over the week end. What was that sentence doing there?

"You are the Entity. Wait for us in your office."

What curious script it was! Not unlike that note he had gotten in some way, but this he could very clearly read. Entity? You are the Entity? What could that be about? Wait in his office? For whom? For what? A sick feeling of impending disaster began to take hold of him. What trick was this? He snatched up an eraser and furiously rubbed back and forth across the message.

At first it would not erase, and then, slowly, when he wiped across the first word, it vanished. Then the second, the third, the fourth! It was erasing now! He finished it so thoroughly that no slightest mark of it was left.

And then, first word, second word, letter by letter with slow cadence, appeared once more. He began to quiver.

Again he grabbed the eraser and rubbed the message out. Slowly, letter by letter, it appeared again.

"You are the Entity. Wait for us in your office."

He flung the eraser away from him just as the first two students entered. He wondered what they would

135

think about the message. Perhaps he could trump up some excuse, include it in the lesson— No, pupils were used to weird statements on blackboards, holdovers from past classes. He had better ignore it completely.

The class shuffled and moved seats and greeted one another the width and length of the room. A girl had a new dress and was being casual. A boy had a new sweetheart and was trying to act very manly in her sight and very careless before his own friends. The rattling and talking and scraping gradually died down. A bell rang. Lowry began his lecture.

Only long habit and much reading from the book carried him through. Now and then, during the hour, his own words came into his consciousness for a moment and he seemed to be talking rationally enough. The students were making notes and dozing and whispering and chewing gum—it was a normal enough class, and obviously they saw nothing wrong.

"This fallacious belief and the natural reluctance of the human being to enter in upon and explore anything so intimately connected with the gods as sickness served as an effective barrier for centuries to any ingress into the realm of medical science. In China—"

Waiting in his office? What could be waiting? And what did it mean, Entity?

"—even when medicinal means were discovered by which fever could be induced or pain lessened, the common people ascribed the fact to the dislike of the demon of illness for that particular herb or the magic qualities of the ritual. Even the doctors themselves long continued certain ritualistic practices, first because they themselves were not sure and because the state of mind of the patient, being a large factor in his possible cure, could be bettered by the apparent flattery of the patient's own beliefs."

It was a relief to be able to stand here and talk to them as though nothing were wrong. And it was a normal class, for they kept gazing through the windows and out of doors, where the sun was bright and friendly and the grass cool and soft.

"In any culture, medical cure begins its history with the thunder of a witch doctor's drums, by which the witch doctor attempts to exorcise his patient." Here he always essayed a small joke about a patient letting himself be cured in a wild effort to save his own eardrums, but just now he could not utter it. Why?—he asked himself.

"Man's predisposition to illness at first acted as a confirmation of spirits and demons, for there was no visible difference, in many cases, between a well patient and a sick one, and what man has not been able to see, he attributes to dev—" He gripped the edge of his lecture desk. "He attributes to devils and demons."

Strange, wasn't it, that medicine drums did cure people? Strange that incantations and health amulets had been man's sole protection from bacteria for generations without count? Strange that medicine itself still retained a multitude of forms which were directly traceable to demons and devils? And that the pile of crutches in that Mexican church indicated the efficacy of faith in even "hopeless" cases. The church! And now that people had turned from the church to a wholly materialistic culture, was it not odd that worldly affairs were so bloody and grim? Demons of hate and devils of destruction, whose lot was to jeer at man and increase his misfortunes! Spirits of the land and water and air, abandoned in belief and left, unhampered, to work their evil upon a world—

He stopped. The class was no longer whispering and chewing gum and staring out the window or dozing. Wide young eyes were fixed upon him in fascination.

He realized that he had spoken his last thoughts aloud. For a moment no longer than an expressive pause would be, he studied his class. Young minds, ready and waiting to be fed anything that any man of repute might wish to feed them, sponges for the half-truths and outright lies and propaganda called education, material to be molded into any shape that their superiors might select. How did he know if he had ever taught truth? He did not even know if the dissemination of democracy itself was error or right. These were the children of the next generation, on the sill of marriage and the legal war of business. Could he, with his background, ever tell them anything which might help them? He, who had been so sure for so many years that all was explainable via material science, he who now had wandered far and had seen things and talked to beings he had for years decried!— could he say now what he had said so often before?

"—and because of that very belief, so deeply rooted in our ancestors, none of us today is sure but what there was some truth in those ancient thoughts. Or perhaps—" Why should he back off now? These were his for the molding. Why should he stand here and lie when not twelve hours ago he had walked with phantoms, had been guided by a priest three hundred and more years dead, had been whipped on by things he had not seen, who even now could catch a glimpse of a black object which threw a shadow where there was no sun? These were his for the molding. Why should he be afraid of them?

"Men of science," he began again in a quiet voice, "have sought to clear fear from the minds of men by telling men that there is nothing of which he must be afraid just because he cannot see the actual cause. Men today have spread the feeling that all things are explained, and that even God himself has had his face gazed upon through the medium of an electric arc. But now, standing here, I am not sure of anything. I have dipped back to find that countless billions of people, all those who lived prior to the last century, regulated their lives with due respect to a supernatural world. Man has always known that his lot upon this earth is misery, and he has, until a split second ago in geological time, understood that there must be beings beyond his ken who take peculiar delight in torturing him.

"In this class at this very moment there are at least half a dozen amulets in which the owner places considerable faith. You call them luck charms and you received them from one beloved or found them through an incident beyond your power of comprehension. You have a semibelief, then, in a goddess of luck. You have a semibelief in a god of disaster. You have all noticed from time to time that at that moment when you felt the most certain of your own invulnerability, that that moment was the beginning of your own downfall. To say aloud that you are never ill seems to invite illness. How many lads have you known who have bragged to you that they have never had accidents, only later to visit them after an accident? And if you did not save some belief in this, then you would not nervously look for wood each time you make a brag about your own fortune.

"This is a modern world, full of material 'explanations,' and yet there is no machine which will guarantee luck; there is no clear statement of any law which serves to regulate man's fate. We know that we face a certain amount of light and, disclaiming any credence in the supernatural or in any existing set of malicious gods, we still understand and clearly that our backs are against the darkness and the void, and that we have a very slight understanding of the amount of misery we are made to experience. We talk about 'breaks,' and we carry luck charms and we knock on wood. We put crosses on top of our churches and arches in our belfries. When one accident has happened, we wait for the other two and only feel at ease when the other two have happened. We place our faiths in a god of good and by that faith carry through, or we go without help through the dim burrows of life, watchful for a demoniac agent of destruction which may rob us of our happiness, or we arrogantly place all faith in ourselves and dare the fates to do their worst. We shiver in the dark. We shudder in the presence of the dead. We look, some of us, to mystic sciences like astrology or numerology to reassure us that our way is clear. And no person in this room, if placed at midnight in a 'haunted' house, would assert there the nonexistence of ghosts. We are intelligent beings, giving our lips to disbelief, but rolling our eyes behind us to search out any danger which might swoop down from that black void.

"Why? Is it true, then, that there exist about us demons and devils and spirits whose jealousy of man leads on to the manufacture of willful harm? Or, despite the evidence of the science of probabilities against the explanation of coincidence, are we to state that mankind brings its misery upon itself? Are there agencies which we generally lack power to perceive?

"As a question only, let me ask, might it not be possible that all of us possess a latent sense which, in our modern scurry, has lapsed in its development? Might not our own ancestors, acute to the primitive dangers, exposed to the wind and the dark, have given attention to the individual development of that sense? And because we have neglected to individually heighten our own perceptions, are we now 'blind' to extra-material agencies? And might we not, at any moment, experience a sudden rebirth of that sense and, as vividly as in a lightning flash, see those things which jealously menace our existences? If we could but see, for ever so brief a period, the supernatural, we would then begin to understand the complexities which beset man. But if we experienced that rebirth and then told of what we saw, might we not be dubbed 'mad'? What of the visions of the saints?

"As children, all of us felt the phantoms of the dark. Might not that sense be less latent in a child whose mind is not yet dulled by the excess burden of facts and facts and more facts? Are there not men in this world today who have converse with the supernatural, but who cannot demonstrate or explain and be believed because of the lack in others of that peculiar sense?

"I am giving you something on which to ponder. You have listened patiently to me for long weeks and you have filled notebooks with scraps of ethnology. I have not once, in all that time until now caused you to think one thought or ponder one question. There is the bell. Think over what I have said."

Half of them, as they wandered out, seemed to think it was one of Professor Lowry's well-known jokes. The other half, of more acute perception, seemed to wonder if Professor Lowry was ill.

Somehow it made no difference to Lowry what they wondered. He had seated himself in his chair and was avoiding all looks by sorting out notes.

"You are the Entity. Wait for us in your office."

CHAPTER

7

He kicked it and it thumped slowly into the corner where its sightless sockets regarded him in mild reproach; one of its teeth had fallen out and made a brown dot on the carpet.

For some time Lowry sat in his office, staring at the disarranged stacks of papers which cluttered his desk, wondering at the way he had finished his lecture. It seemed to him, as he thought about it, that man's lot seems to be a recanting of statement and prejudice; those things which he most wildly vows he will not do are those things which, eventually, he must do; those beliefs which are the most foreign to his nature are eventually thrust down his throat by a malignant fate. To think that he, James Lowry, ethnologist, would ever come near a recognition of extra-sensory forces— Well, here he was, waiting. Waiting for what?

Those four hours?

The thought made him rise and pace around the room with the hunched manner of a jungle brute surrounded by bars. He caught himself at it and forced calmness by stirring various bundles with his foot and looking at the address labels of the things which had been shipped up from Yucatan. There was a year's work at this classification, and even he did not know what he had here. Bits of stone, pieces of rubble, plaster casts of prints, hasty miniatures of idols, a scroll in a metal container—

To fill his waiting he unwrapped the first box at hand and set it on his desk. He lifted the cover from it. It was just a fossilized skull found beside a sacrificial block, the last relic of some poor devil who had had his heart torn, living, from his body to satisfy the priest-imagined craving of some brutal deity whose life was thought to need renewal. Just a brown, sightless skull— He had dug this out quite cold-bloodedly, so used he had

147

become to his job. Why did it make him shudder so now?

His name—that was it. That must be it! His name engraved upon that headstone.

JAMES LOWRY
Born 1901
Died 1940
Rest In Peace

Odd that he should somehow fall upon the grassy mound of his own grave; odder still that it would be the one place he had found rest that night. And the date? 1940?

He swallowed a dry lump which threatened to cut off his breathing. "This year?" Tomorrow, next week, next month?

Died 1940

And he had found rest from his torment.

The door opened and Tommy came in. Lowry knew who it was, but he could not quite bring himself to look at Tommy's face. And when he did, as his eyes swept up he saw the malevolent smile and those yellow fangs. But when he looked straight at Tommy it was the same Tommy he had always known.

"So life is too dull for you," said Tommy with a smile. "You wouldn't want to send up to Chemistry for some nitroglycerin, would you? Or do you need it?"

"What's wrong?"

"Nothing wrong, except that one of your students nearly collapsed from hysteria. And the rest of them—or some of them, at least—are walking around muttering to themselves about demons and devils. Don't tell me you are seeing things my way now."

"Not your way," said Lowry. "What a man sees he is forced to believe."

"Well, well, well, old Witch Doctor Lowry himself! Do you actually think those things they say you said?"

"What else can I think? For forty-eight hours I have walked and talked, pursued and been pursued by phantoms."

"You seem quite calm about it."

"Why shouldn't I be calm?"

"Oh, no reason. You seem much less agitated than you have been the past few days, or Saturday and Sunday, to be exact. Is . . . well, do you still see—"

"It's there," said Lowry. "A man can get used to anything."

The door opened a second time and they turned to see Mary. She was oblivious of any stir Lowry might have made in class, and had no anxiety to question him, evidently feeling that she might possibly be the cause of some of his strange actions. She looked half frightened now for all that she was smiling, and then, seeing Lowry smile at her, she brightened.

"Hello, Jim. Hello, Tommy. I just breezed by for a very wifely reason, Jim. The exchequer, much as I hate to mention it, is at a very low ebb, and spring and an empty larder demand some clothes and some groceries."

Jim pulled out his checkbook.

"That," said Tommy, "is the reason I'll never marry."

149

"It's a pleasure," said Lowry, writing out the check.

"It's two hours to my next class," said Tommy. "May I be burdened with your bundles?"

"Such a delightful beast of burden is quite acceptable," said Mary with a curtsy.

Lowry gave her the check and she kissed him lightly. Tommy took her arm and they left the office.

Was it some sort of sensory illusion that caused Lowry to momentarily feel fangs in her mouth? Was it some way the light fell upon her face that made him see those fangs? Was it a natural jealousy which made him believe she looked lovingly at Tommy as they went out of the door?

He shook his head violently in an effort to clear away such horrible thoughts, and turned to his desk to find himself face to face with the skull. Angrily, he put the top upon the box and cast it away from him; but the top did not stay on, nor did the box remain atop the pile of packages; the skull rolled with a hollow sound and finally stood on its nose hole against his foot. He kicked it and it thumped slowly into the corner where its sightless sockets regarded him in mild reproach; one of its teeth had fallen out and made a brown dot on the carpet.

JAMES LOWRY

Born 1901

Died 1940

Rest In Peace

His thoughts had gotten all tangled until he could not remember if this was Sebastian's skull or not, or even if Sebastian's grave had yielded anything but dust and a golden belt. Aimlessly, from the depths of his high-school cramming, came the words, "To be or not to be, that is the question." He said them over several times before he recognized them at all. He essayed, then, a sort of grim joke, muttering, "Alas, poor Lowry. I knew him, Horatio—"

He tried to laugh at himself and failed. He could feel his nerves tautening again; he could hear the echoes of the old mother's remarks. Cats, hats, rats— Cats, hats, rats. Hats, bats, cats, rats. Hats lead to bats, lead to cats, lead to rats. Rats are hungry, James Lowry. Rats will eat you, James Lowry. Hats, you came here to bats, you go on to cats, you get eaten by rats. Do you still want to find your hat? Hats, bats, cats, rats. Rats are hungry, James Lowry. Rats will eat you, James Lowry.

Rats will eat you, James Lowry.

Rats will eat you, James Lowry.

Rats will eat you, James Lowry.

Rats will eat you, James Lowry.

Rats will eat you, James Lowry.

Rats will eat you, James Lowry.

Rats will eat you, James Lowry.

Do you still want to find your hat?

Do you still want to find your hat?

DO YOU STILL WANT TO FIND YOUR HAT?

He threw himself away from the desk and crashed his chair to the floor. The sound of violence gave him some relief, but the second he picked it up—

Hats, bats, rats, cats. Hats, bats, cats, rats. Hats, hats, hats. Bats, bats, bats, bats. Rats, rats, rats, rats, rats. Hats, bats, cats, hats, rats, hats, bats, rats, cats, hats, rats, bats, cats—

Do you still want to find your hat, James Lowry?

"No!"

"Then," said a childish treble, "you are the Entity."

He glared around his office in search of the owner of the voice. But the office was empty.

And then Lowry saw a certain movement on the wall before his desk where a bookcase had been taken away, leaving a meaningless pattern of scars upon the plaster. He stared at the place intently and found that it was taking definite shape. First the vague outline of a face, and then, little by little, an extension which began to form as a body. Hair came into being upon the head, and the eyes moved slightly and a hand emerged from the wall to be followed by the rest.

"I would dislike frightening you," said the high, musical voice.

The thing looked like a child not more than four years old, a little girl with long blond curls and shapely, dimpled limbs. She was dressed in a frilled frock, all clean and white, and a white bow was slightly to one side of her head. Her face was round and beautiful, but it was a strange kind of beauty, not altogether childish; the eyes were such a dark blue they were almost black, and deep in them was an expression which was not an innocent child's, but more a lascivious wanton's; the lips were full and rich and slightly parted, as though to bestow a greedy lover's kiss. And like an aura a black shadow stood in globular shape about her. But at a casual, swift glance, it was a little child, no more than four, naive and full of laughter. The lewd eyes lingered caressingly upon Lowry's face as she perched herself upon the top of his desk.

"No, I do not frighten you, do I?"

"What . . . what are you?" said Lowry.

"Why, a child, of course. Have you no eyes?" And pensively, then, "You know, you are a very handsome-looking man, Mr. Lowry. So big and rough—" A dreamy look came into her eyes and her small pink tongue flicked out to dampen her lips convulsively.

"You wrote that message?"

"No. But I come to tell you about it. You are quite sure now, Mr. Lowry, that you do not want to find your hat?"

"*No!*"

"It was a very pretty hat."

"I never want to see it again."

She smiled and leaned back languorously, her little shoes making occasional thumps against the side of the desk. She yawned and stretched and then looked long at him. The full little lips quivered and the pink tongue flicked. With a seeming effort she brought herself to business.

"If you are through with all such nonsense and disbelief in us," she began, "and if you will aid us against the *others*, then I shall tell you something you should be glad to hear. Are you?"

Lowry hesitated and then nodded. He felt very weary.

"You visited your friend, Tommy Williams, just before you lost your four hours, didn't you?"

"You probably know more about it than I," said Lowry with bitterness.

For a moment she laughed, and Lowry started as he recognized the sound which had been near him so many hours. He looked studiously at her and found that her image seemed to pulsate and that the black aura expanded and contracted like some great unclean thing breathing.

She swung her little princess slippers against the desk and continued. "Tommy Williams told you the truth. You offered us a challenge and said we did not exist, and we know more about you than you do. You see, all this was scheduled, anyway. Every few generations, Mr. Lowry, we even up accounts with mankind. Such a period has just begun. And you, Mr. Lowry, are invested with control, for we must have a human control."

She smiled and dimples appeared in her soft cheeks. She smoothed out her dress with little-girl gestures, and then, looking at him, she drummed her heels.

"That is what we mean by 'Entity,' Mr. Lowry. You are the Entity, the center of control. Usually all life, at fleeting instants, takes turns in passing this along. Now perhaps you have, at one time in your life, had a sudden feeling, 'I am I'? Well, that awareness of yourself is akin to what men call godliness. For an instant nearly every living thing in this world has been the one Entity, the focal point for all life. It is like a torch being passed from hand to hand. Usually, innocent little children such as myself are invested, and so it is that a child ponders much upon his own identity."

"What are you trying to tell me?"

"Why," she said demurely, "I am telling you that this is a period when *we* choose an Entity and invest that function in just one man. Your Tommy Williams, I believe, knows about it. So long as you live, then the world is animated. So long as you walk and hear and see, the world goes forward. In your immediate vicinity, you understand, all life is concentrating upon demonstrating that it is alive. It is not. Others are only props for you. This would have happened to you a long time ago, but it was difficult to achieve communication with you. You are the Entity, the only living thing in this world."

The globe of darkness around her pulsated gently. She touched her dainty little hands to her white hair ribbon and then folded them in her lap. She looked fixedly at Lowry, and that slow look of the wanton came into her eyes and her lips parted a little. Her breath quickened.

"What . . . what am I expected to do?" said Lowry.

"Why, nothing. You are the Entity."

"H-he-e i-is-s t-th-he-e E-En-n-ti-it-ty!" growled a chorus of voices in other parts of the room.

"But why do you tell me?"

"So that nothing will worry you, and so that you will do nothing rash. You are afraid of Tommy Williams. Well, Tommy Williams, as well as Jebson and Billy Watkins, is just a prop which you motivate yourself."

"Then how is it that this morning he came to me and leaned over me and stared at my face and I could not move?"

She tensed. "What is this he did?"

"Just stared into my face. And I keep seeing fangs when I don't look at him directly—"

"Oh!" she cried in shocked pain. "Then it is impossible!"

"I-it-t i-is-s i-im-mp-po-os-si-i-b-bl-le-e!" chorused the growls.

"It's too late," she stated finally. "There is nothing you can do. Tommy Williams is the leader of the *others*. And you must somehow settle accounts with Tommy Williams."

"Why?"

"He has already taken from you a part of your soul substance."

"He was here just a few minutes ago."

"Every time he sees you he'll try to take some! You must prevent it!"

"How?" cried Lowry.

But the little child was gone, and the black aura

turned darker and began to vanish at the top until it seemed like a small, round black thing. With a smoke puff it was gone!

"How?" shouted Lowry.

Only the echo of his own voice against his own walls answered him. And when he fixed his eyes upon the broken spot in the plaster, it was just a broken spot with no resemblance whatever to either a face or anything else.

What had that thing been?

Where was it now?

Lowry buried his face in his arms.

When the twelve-o'clock bell rang, Lowry got up more from force of habit than from any wish to leave his office. A gnawing ache of apprehension was suffused through his being as though he subconsciously expected a blow to smash him at any moment from the least expected quarter. With effort he put the feeling down; he squared his shoulders and slipped into his topcoat and strode forth with watchful eyes. But there was another feeling which was gradually coming toward recognition in him, a feeling that nothing could touch him. And as the first one was stamped out, the second one rose. It was not unlike a religious fanatic's trust in a personally interested god, a thing which seemed very foreign to Lowry. And as he walked through the hurrying crowds of students in the halls and down the stairs, he began to be conscious of his own size and strength.

He was, after all, a big fellow, but, being of a very shy nature, he had never taken much notice of the fact, thinking of his person, rather, as being somewhat underweight and undersize—without really thinking about the matter at all. Some of the athletes of the college came past him in a group, and he noticed, almost smiling, that he was taller and heavier than they. Odd he had never taken that personal quality of his into account. It was like finding a gold mine or having a beautiful woman suddenly confess her love, or hearing a million people stand up and cheer themselves into exhaustion for one.

Outside, a student had taken a seat upon the steps so that the penetrating languor of sunlight could caress his back; in his hands he held a newspaper. As Lowry passed him he wondered for a moment what was going on in the world and so glanced at the sheet.

For an instant he wondered if he were going blind.

There wasn't any printing on the paper.

It was just a white sheet, but for all that the student seemed to be reading it with avidity!

Lowry, troubled a little, went on. But as he walked, the exhilaration of exercise restored the pleasant feeling within him, and he gradually forgot about the newspaper. Several small groups of students were standing along the walk, chattering among themselves. A man was pushing a lawn mower industriously. A boy was trotting along with the yellow telegraph envelope in his hand.

Suddenly Lowry had a strange feeling about things, as though something was happening behind him which he should know about. He stopped and whirled around.

The boy had stopped trotting, but started instantly. The man at the lawn mower had paused but was now mowing again. The little crowds of students had ceased gesticulating and laughing for the smallest fraction of time but instantly went to it once more.

Lowry pondered the matter as he walked on. Perhaps there was something happening in his head, like false memory. Certainly it was just his imagination which led him to believe that things had paused outside his observation.

Old Billy Watkins, up earlier than usual, came limping by. He paused and touched his cap. "You feelin' better today, Ji—Professor Lowry?"

"Much better, thanks."

"Well, take care of yourself, Jim—Professor Lowry."

"Thanks, Billy."

Lowry walked on, and then again he had that feeling. He stopped and looked over his shoulder. Old Billy Watkins was standing like a limp scarecrow, but as soon as Lowry really noticed it, Old Billy went on swinging down the street. And the man at the lawn mower and the messenger and the students—they had all stopped, too, only to resume under Lowry's glance.

That was very strange, thought Lowry.

And something else which was strange awaited him when he continued on his way. A horse-drawn cart had been plodding along on his right, and both the horse and the cart had paused in mid-action when he looked away, only to start plodding along again under his scrutiny.

He had reached the small café where the professors generally took their luncheon. He opened the door upon silence. No clatter of knives and forks, no rattle of dishes, no jangle of talking. Silence. But only for an instant. Lowry stepped into the café and the rattling and clattering and jangling started in full blast like a sound track clipped on halfway through. Other than that there was nothing unusual about the place. Other professors called to him in greeting, and the sprinkling of students nodded politely, and he was forced into a chair.

"Damn shame what Jebson did to you," said a young professor in disgust. Somebody evidently kicked him, for a spasm of pain went across his face to be swiftly erased. "I still think it's a shame."

"Chicken salad sandwich and a glass of milk," said Lowry to the waiter.

He talked, then, with the men at his table about the petty subjects of the campus and told them an anecdote about his latest trip to Yucatan. The feeling of self-possession, coupled with an "allness" of being, put him quite at ease. And a little later, when they were breaking up, he was aware of the fact that he had made his friendship with these fellows a little closer. But there had been something odd about this place all during lunch. He had, several times, attempted to listen in upon the talk at the table behind him, but it had all been sounds; just a jumble of sounds.

It occurred to him that this was Monday and he

experienced a feeling of relief. He would not have to lecture again today; for his heavy days were Tuesday and Thursday. He could go out and walk around and enjoy the clear sunshine and forget about these things which had happened to him.

The place was almost empty when he left. He stood for a second outside the door, wondering which way he should go. And then it struck him that all was not well with this familiar street.

Two cars were at a standstill in the traffic lane, their drivers apparently asleep over their wheels. A kid on a bike was leaning inertly against a tree. Three students were slumped at the curb.

These people must be dead!

But no. No, the drivers were sitting up straight now and the cars were getting in motion. The kid on the bike was pedaling away in a rush. The three students grabbed up their books and casually strolled toward the campus.

Lowry turned around and looked inside the café. The cashier was sprawled over the glass case beside the register. A waiter was poised in the middle of the room with one foot in the air and a tray of dishes balanced on his palm. A late diner was almost face down in his soup. Lowry took an inadvertent step toward them.

The waiter began to move smoothly. The cashier scribbled at a pad. The late diner began to make a great deal of noise over the soup.

Puzzled, Lowry turned away from the college and went on down the street. What was happening to him now?

He stopped at a newsdealer's stand and bought a paper. There was nothing wrong with the newsdealer, for the old man did his usual trick of stalling to keep the customer from asking for the two pennies change he should get.

Discarding the evidences he had witnessed, Lowry went along. He looked at the paper. It did not particularly amaze him that this one, too, was blank, but he felt a kindling of wrath against the newsdealer. He whirled and marched back to the stand. Another man had been standing there buying a paper, but now both the customer and the newsdealer were without motion, slumped across the stand. They did not go into action until Lowry was almost upon them and then, casually, they transacted their business. But Lowry noticed that the customer's paper was also blank. Disgustedly, Lowry tossed his own paper upon the street and returned to his way.

Lowry wandered along in a northerly direction, taking a course which would soon lead him out of town; for he felt a craving for the quieting comfort of a stream in which he had long ago swum and the sound of a breeze in the willows which flanked it. Other manifestations, just enough apparent to make him wonder at them, were met on the way, people and beasts and birds which went into action a moment late. He was convinced that he was seeing late or that his mind, being wearied by the events of the two days past, was not registering instantaneously. He did not much worry until he reached the place where he had intended to rest. It had occurred to him belatedly that the spot was now the site of a cellulose factory; but, as he approached, no sign of factory or factory smoke was marring the sky.

He found the place beside the pool in which he used to dive in defiance of a sign which read: "City Water Supply. Do Not Contaminate." He stretched himself out in the cool grass and felt the sun upon him. How satisfying it was to come here and yet how different he was from the boy who had lazed in this cover throughout the long vacations. Little by little he slipped into a languorous happiness and idly reviewed the things he had thought and done as a kid in overalls. Then he had been in awe of his father, and now he was as his father had been, a professor at Atworthy.

The thought amused him that he was the image of his own early awe, and he dwelt at length upon what he would have said to the boy in overalls who had lain long hours in this very spot, how he would have told him that the mystery of the elder world was no mystery at all, but an uncertain sort of habit of dignity, perhaps grown out of the image of youth, perhaps as an excuse for diminished physical vigor, perhaps as a handy shield by which one could hold off the world. How little that boy need have worried, after all. The state of being "grown up" was a state beset by as many worries, and just as false, as those of childhood.

After a little he became aware of a swift hammering sound and the snarl of a truck engine. He tried to put the invasion aside, but it persisted and grew in volume and activity until his curiosity was aroused. What was going on in this vicinity?

He got up and peered through the willows, catching a glimpse of a half-finished wall. What was that? He moved out of hiding and was astonished to see two hundred or more workmen carrying materials and hammering nails and laying bricks with a speed which excelled anything he had ever before seen. A factory was going up a foot at a time, yard, mud, tanks, stacks, wire gates and all! And what a sweat of rushing! He drifted nearer and was conscious of the eyes of workmen upon him. The men, as soon as they glimpsed him, looked bewildered. A foreman began to bray curses at them. And within a minute, the factory was done. The workmen promptly dived in through the doors and came out bearing lunch boxes and then, as though this was wrong, the foreman flayed into them anew and a whistle blew and a siren whooped and the workmen sped inside again to send out a great clamor of machinery and the roar of steam. The plant was going full blast. The willows had vanished. The stream of yesterday was a concrete aqueduct!

Dazed, Lowry turned his back upon the place and strode swiftly back toward the town. He was beginning to feel a nausea of concern about these events. How did his own appearance so affect conditions?

The world continued to lag for him as he entered the town. People were still until he was in sight and then they moved, just as if they were props in an artificial scene.

A suspicion took form in him and he suddenly changed his course. What about all these houses?

What about them?

When he got halfway down a block that he had never traversed in his memory, he stepped abruptly into an alleyway.

Just as he had expected. These houses had fronts but no backs! They were sets!

He went on down the alley and here and there people made belated attempts to complete the false fronts and give them false backs, but they were fumbling and bewildered, as though Lowry's presence and appearance set their knees to knocking.

What of the main street? He had never been in many of the stores. Feeling he had to put this thing to complete test, he hurried along, unmindful of the effect he seemed to have upon these puppets.

He rounded a block of the main thoroughfare of the town, but just before he turned the corner a terror-stricken voice reached him:

"Jim! Jim! Jim! Oh, my God! *Jim!*"

He leaped around the corner and halted, appalled. The whole avenue was littered with apparently dead people. They were sprawled against steering wheels and in the gutters. They were leaning stiffly against store fronts. The traffic cop was a rag draped about his signal. A two-horse team was down in the traces and the farmer on the box was canted over, slack-jawed as a corpse. And through this tangled carpet of props ran Mary. Her hat was gone and her hair was wild and her eyes were dilated with horror.

He called to her and she almost fell with relief. Sobbing, arms outstretched, she threw herself upon him and buried a tear-streaked face upon his breast.

"Jim!" she sobbed. "Oh, my God! Jim!"

As he smoothed down her hair with a gentle hand, he watched the street come to life and resume the petty activity with which he was so familiar. The cop blew his whistle and swung his signal, and the horses leaped up and began to pull, and the farmer took a chew and spat. Buyers and sellers bought and sold and there was not one thing wrong with the whole street. But Jim knew that if he looked behind him those people who now passed him would be stopped again, slumped, their puppet strings slack.

A familiar figure swung along toward them. Tommy, swinging a limber black stick, his hat on the back of his head and his handsome face with its customary quirk of amusement, approached them and paused in recognition.

"Hello, Jim." And then, in concern, "Is something wrong with Mary?"

"You know what's wrong with Mary, Tom Williams."

Tommy looked at him oddly. "I don't get you, old man."

"Not that you wouldn't try," said Jim with a cold grin at his own humor. "I've had enough of this."

"Enough of what?"

"You took something from me. I want it back. I know about this, you see."

"Well?"

"I want that part of myself back."

"You accuse me—"

"Of being a thief?"

"Well?"

"So long as I had all of myself, all was well in this world. Now that part of me is gone—"

Tommy laughed amusedly. "So you've caught on, have you?"

"And I'll remedy this, Tom Williams, or put an end to you."

Tommy's laugh was brittle and he swung the cane as though he would like to strike out with it. "How is it that you rate so much?"

"I don't know or care how it is. What is mine is mine. Give me back that part of myself, Tom Williams."

"And lose my own?" said Tommy with a smile.

"What is mine is mine," said Lowry.

"I believe in a more communistic attitude," said Tommy. "I happen to want that part of you and I certainly intend to keep it." And now the fangs at the corners of his mouth were quite plain.

Lowry put Mary to one side. He snatched out and grabbed Tommy's coat and hauled him close, aiming a blow. Somehow, Tommy twisted from the grasp and, in his turn, struck hard with his cane. For an instant the world, for Lowry, was ink. But he came up in an effort to lunge at Tommy's throat. Again the cane felled him. Stunned now, he swayed on his hands and knees, trying to clear his fogged senses. Once more the cane struck him and he felt the pavement strike against his cheek.

In a little while he was conscious of a face close to his own, a face from which protruded yellow fangs. A sick weakness, as though he was bleeding to death, pinned him to the walk.

Tommy stood up straight and Lowry found that he could not move. Tommy seemed twice as big and strong as before.

Mary looked at Tommy for a long while, the expression of her face slowly changing from one of wonder to one of agreeable satisfaction. And then Lowry knew why it was. She was nothing but a puppet herself, animated more than any of the rest because she had been more with a source. And when Tommy had taken part of him she had begun to divide her attention between them, for either one could animate her. And now that Tommy possessed an "allness" there could be no question as to which one she would follow.

She gave no glance at all at Lowry on the walk. She looked up into Tommy's face and smiled tenderly. Tommy smiled back and, arm in arm, they walked away.

Lowry tried to shout after them, but they paid no heed. They were gone around the corner.

By degrees, then, the street began to slump and

become still. By degrees, but not wholly. Here and there a puppet twitched a little. Here and there a mouth made motions without making sound. Lowry stared in terror at the scene.

For him the world was nearly dead!

His body was so heavy that he could scarcely move at all. But he knew that he must pursue them, find them, gain back that vital force which had been stolen. To live, an eighth alive, in a world of apparent dead would drive him mad!

And Mary!

How could— But she was just a puppet, too. A puppet with all the rest. It was no fault of hers. The guilt was all Tommy's. Tommy that he had thought his friend!

It was agony to drag himself along, but he did, inch by inch, fumbling over the bodies which lay sprawled in the clear sunlight. He became aware of how hot it was getting and of a great weariness. If he could just rest for a little while, he might be able to find strength. He saw a bush in a yard where the cover was thick and he crawled into the coolness. Just to rest a little while and then to find Tommy and Mary!

CHAPTER

8

Each face into which he looked in turn became Tommy's! And each face possessed that mocking smile and slyly evil glint of eye.

It was nearly dusk when he awoke. He stretched himself stiffly, for he had become cold. For a moment he could not recall the events which had passed, and he came to his knees, aware of a thing he must do but not quite able to place it. This lethargy! Was it affecting his brain as well?

But no, his brain was all right. Yes! Tommy and Mary and the world of the apparent dead!

And what a tremendous amount of good that rest had done him. Or else—

He peered forth from the bushes. There were people walking along the street and so it was fairly plain that Tommy would be somewhere nearby and that Lowry himself was drawing some of the force in common with the other puppets. Perhaps that would help him! If he could get close to Tommy and then, supported by Tommy's own effect, he could possibly win back what he had lost.

He lurked in the shadows of the street, watching for Tommy. But no, he could not locate any sign of him. Could it be that Tommy was in one of these houses? Perhaps dining? In such a position that he might look out and see the street?

Perhaps there was another explanation. Perhaps, now that Tommy had all of it, these puppets would go on with their make-believe lives and Lowry along with them. But he himself knew and they—

He emerged from cover. There was a man standing beside the letter box on the corner. Maybe he would know where to find Tommy. Lowry, assuming a careless air, sauntered up to the fellow. He was about to open his mouth and begin to question when his heart lurched within.

This was Tommy!

Tommy, with a mocking smile upon his mouth and a sly look in his eye!

Lowry whirled and sped away, but when he found that no footsteps followed he slowed down. He glanced back and the man on the corner was looking after him and there was light, cheerful laughter suspended in the air.

Why wasn't he able to face him? Did he have to find him sleeping in order to steal away that which he had lost?

Lowry stopped. Couldn't he be more clever about this? Couldn't he perhaps explain to some of these puppets what had happened to the world and thereby gain help? Many of them could assail Tommy and weigh him down and take that from him which rightfully belonged to the world.

He went along, looking for someone to whom he could broach the plan. A man was watering a lawn inside a picket fence and Lowry stopped and beckoned to him. The man, holding the hose, strolled languidly over.

Lowry was about to begin when he looked into the fellow's face. Despite the dusk that face was plain!

It was Tommy!

Lowry whirled and ran, and again the light laughter hung upon the evening air.

He slowed down, stubbornly refusing to be panicked. There was no use losing his head, for he still had a chance. Not everyone could be Tommy.

Soon he saw a woman hurrying homeward. If he told her and she told her husband— Yes. He would stop her.

He held up his hand and she dodged from him, but seeing no menace in him she allowed him to speak. He had uttered just one word when he saw who she was.

Mary!

His heart skipped a beat. Here she was alone! And he could plead with her— Again he started to speak. But Mary's face was full of scorn and she turned her back upon him and walked away.

It took Lowry some seconds to get over that. But he would not admit defeat. Here came three students. Students would obey him certainly, and these fellows wore sweaters with stripes around the arm. He stepped out in front of them.

When they had stopped and were looking at him, he started to speak. And then he stopped. Each face into which he looked in turn became Tommy's! And each face possessed that mocking smile and slyly evil glint of eye.

Lowry stepped back and kept on walking backward. He spun about and ran away and did not stop until he had come to the cover of the next block.

A woman was there, but he knew better than to halt her, for even at ten feet, by the light of the street lamp, he could see that she was Mary. He pulled his hat ashamedly down over his eyes and slouched by and then, when she was going away from him, he began to run once more.

He fled past other pedestrians, and each one that

looked at him was possessed of the face of either Tommy or Mary. And after a little they began to call to him at intervals.

"Hello, Jim," said Tommy in mockery each time.

"Oh, it's you, Jim," said Mary.

Thickening dark and the thin street lamps' glowing oppressed Lowry. It was becoming warmer by degrees and then, swiftly, turned cold. The house fronts were chill and impassive in the gloom; their lighted windows like glowing eyes that looked at him and mocked.

"Hello, Jim."

And again, "Oh, it's you, Jim."

Spreading lawns and the huddled shapes of bushes peopled the night with strange phantoms. Little shadows raced about his feet and sometimes brushed against his legs with a soft, furry touch. Once, as he stepped down from a curb, he saw a scaly thing dissolve an instant late.

And then Tommy's face, all by itself, floated eerily against the gray dark. The thing was thin and blurry, but the smile was there and the sly eyes regarded him steadily. The face faded away and left only the glinting of the eyes.

Before him a shape had begun to dance, pausing until he almost caught up to it and then scurrying to get out of reach, to dance again and beckon. There was a certain mannerism about it that brought its identity to him. Wearily he recognized Mary, her face cold in scorn.

Why and where was she leading him?

"Hello, Jim."

"Oh, it's you, Jim."

Shadows and the gloomy fronts of houses coldly staring. Shadows on the lawns and hiding at the edges of trees. Soft things which bumped his legs and a great shadow like spread wings reaching out to engulf the whole of the town.

Blurry white wisps of faces drifting just ahead. Tommy's and Mary's. Mary's and Tommy's.

Above, there was a rustling as of bats. Below, there came up a low and throaty sound. And the smells of fresh-cut grass and growing things were tinged with a perfume he could not define. A perfume. As illusive as those faces which drifted ever before him. A perfume— Mary's. Mary's perfume. Mingled with the smell of exotic tobacco. Exotic tobacco. Tommy's.

The great dark cloud spread and spread and the lamps became dim and the shadows deepened and began to march jerkily beside him at a distance. Each shadow, stationary until he came to it, coming up and marching with the rest. Darker and darker and then no sounds at all. No sounds or smells. Just the thin wisp of a mocking smile, gradually fading, forever receding.

Weakly he leaned against the parapet of a little stone bridge behind the church and listened to the water saying: "Oh, it's you, Jim." "Hello, Jim."

At the other end there stood a dark, thick shadow. A thing with a slouch hat upon its head and a black cloak draped about it which reached down to its buckled shoes.

It was carefully braiding a rope, strand by strand. Lowry knew he would rest a little and then walk over the bridge to the man of darkness.

"Oh, it's you, Jim."

"Hello, Jim."

Quiet little rippling voices, almost unheard, slowly fading. And now there was nothing more of that smile. There was nothing in the sky but the vast shadow and the plaintive whimper of an evening wind.

The street lamp threw a pale light upon him and by its light he tried to see the water. The voices down there were scarcely whispers now, only a rippling murmur, a kind and soothing sound.

He caught a glimpse of something white in the water and leaned a trifle farther, not particularly interested in the fact that it was a reflection of his own face in the black mirror surface below. He watched the image grow clearer, watched his own eyes and mouth take form. It was as if he was seeing himself down there, a self far more real than this self leaning against cold stone. Idly he beckoned to the image. It seemed to grow nearer. He beckoned again in experiment. It was nearer still.

With sudden determination he held out both hands to it. It was gone from the water, but it was not gone.

Jim Lowry stood up straight. He took a long, deep breath of the fresh evening air and looked up at the stars in the sky. He turned and looked along the avenue and saw people strolling and enjoying the smell of fresh-cut grass. He looked across the bridge and saw Old Billy Watkins leaning against a stone, puffing contentedly upon a pipe.

With a feeling that was almost triumph, for all the weight of sorrow within him, Jim Lowry crossed the bridge and approached the night policeman.

"Oh. Hello, Professor Lowry."

"Hello, Billy."

"Nice night."

"Yes . . . yes, Billy. A nice night. I want you to do something for me, Billy."

"Anything, Jim."

"Come with me."

Old Billy knocked the ashes from his pipe and silently fell in beside. Old Billy was a wise old fellow. He could feel Lowry's mood and he said nothing to intrude upon it, merely walked along smelling the growing things of spring.

They walked for several blocks and then Jim Lowry turned into the path at Tommy's house. The old mansion was unlighted and still and seemed to be waiting for them.

"You should have a key to fit that door, Billy."

"Yes. I've got one; it's a common lock."

Old Billy turned the knob and fumbled for the hall light, turning it on and standing back to follow Lowry.

Jim Lowry pointed at the hatrack in the hall and indicated a lady's bag which lay there beside a lady's hat. There was another hat there, a man's, trammeled, halfway between hatrack and living room; it had initials in the band, "J. L."

"Come with me, Billy," said Jim Lowry in a quiet, controlled voice. As they passed the living room, Old Billy saw the stumps of a broken chair and an upset ash tray.

Jim Lowry held the kitchen door open and turned on the light. The window was broken there.

A mewling sound came from somewhere and Jim Lowry opened the door to the cellar. With steady, slow steps he descended a short flight of stairs, through newly swung strands of cobwebs. A Persian cat with a half-mad look bolted past them and fled out of the house.

Jim fumbled for the basement light. For a moment it seemed that he would not turn it on, but that was only for a moment. The naked bulb flooded the basement and filled it with sharp, swinging shadows.

A crude hole had been dug in the middle of the dirt floor and a shovel was abandoned beside it.

Jim Lowry took hold of the light cord and lifted it so that the rays would stream into the coal bin.

An ax, black with blood, pointed its handle at them. From the coal protruded a white something.

Old Billy stepped to the dark, dusty pile and pushed some of the lumps away. A small avalanche rattled, disclosing the smashed and hacked face of Tommy Williams. To his right, head thrown back, staring eyes fixed upon the stringers and blood-caked arm outflung, lay the body of Mary, Jim Lowry's wife.

Old Billy looked for several minutes at Jim Lowry and then Jim Lowry spoke, his voice monotonous. "I did it Saturday afternoon. And Saturday night I came back here to find the evidence I had left—my hat—and dispose of the bodies. Sunday I came again—I had to climb in the window. I'd lost the key."

Jim Lowry sank down upon a box and hid his face in his palms. "I don't know why I did it. Oh, God, forgive me, I don't know why. I found her here, hiding, after I had found her hat. Everything was whirling and I couldn't hear what they kept screaming at me and . . . and I killed them." A sob shook him. "I don't know why. I don't know why she was here . . . I don't know why I could not reason . . . cerebral malaria . . . jealous madness—"

Old Billy moved a little and the coal pile shifted and rattled. Tommy's arm was bared. It seemed to thrust itself toward Lowry, and in the cold fist was clenched a scrap of paper as though mutely offering explanation even in death.

Old Billy removed the paper and read:

TOMMY OLD SPORT:

Next week is Jim's birthday and I want to surprise him with a party. I'll come over Saturday afternoon and you can help me make up the list of his friends and give me your expert advice on the demon rum. Don't let him know a word of this.

Regards,

MARY

Somewhere high above, there seemed to hang a tinkle

of laughter: high, amused laughter, gloating and mocking and evil.

Of course, though, it was probably just the sigh of wind whining below the cellar door.

ABOUT THE AUTHOR

Born in 1911, the son of a U.S. naval officer, the legendary L. Ron Hubbard grew up in the great American West and was acquainted early with a rugged outdoor life before he took to sea. The cowboys, Indians and wide-open spaces of Montana were soon balanced with an open ocean, ancient temples, and the throngs of the Orient that he saw as a teenager. By the age of nineteen, he had travelled over a quarter of a million miles, recording what he saw in a series of diaries mixed with story ideas.

Returning to the U.S., his insatiable curiosity and demand for excitement took him to the sky as a barnstormer, where he quickly earned a reputation for skill and daring.

Then he returned to the high seas, this time aboard a four-masted schooner, leading expeditions through the Caribbean, where he found still more adventure that would serve him later at the typewriter.

Drawing from his travels, and his first-hand experience with 21 different races and cultures, he produced an amazing wealth of stories: air, land and sea adventures; westerns; detective; mystery; a broad catalogue of entertainment that enthralled his ever-expanding readership.

As with leading fiction writers of the era, Ron was invited to Hollywood in 1937, where he soon left his mark, writing such popular screenplays as Columbia's box office serial hit, "THE SECRET OF TREASURE ISLAND."

In 1938, the publishing empire of Street and Smith, Inc., concerned over the flagging sales of its major magazine, "Astounding Science Fiction," called for a fresh approach from the country's top adventure writers. Although intrigued with the prospect of writing science fiction. L. Ron Hubbard protested that he did not write about "machines and machinery"—he wrote about people. "That's just what we want," he was told. History was made as a result.

The upshot of Street and Smith's inspiration was a cornucopia of L. Ron Hubbard stories that expanded the scope of the genre, and gained him lasting high repute as a founding father of the great Golden Age of science fiction.

Ron went beyond science fiction by tantalizing readers with exciting new fantasy. Responding to this demand, Street and Smith launched "Unknown" magazine, to accommodate the developing fantasy market.

It was in the July, 1940, issue of "Unknown" that FEAR first appeared, startling the readership and setting a new standard for horror fiction. Author Ray Bradbury commented that this story was a landmark in his own writing career and he was so taken by FEAR that he even had actors perform it as a radio play. Without doubt, it is the single most remembered story from "Unknown."

World War II came and L. Ron Hubbard was called to duty. Entering U.S. naval service in mid-1941, by the end of that decade he was no longer writing fiction, his experiences with war having impressed on him the deep need to research the underlying causes of Man's inhumanity to Man. For the next 32 years, he researched, wrote and published millions of words of nonfiction concerning the nature of Man.

In 1982, however, to celebrate his 50th anniversary as a professional author, he wrote the international blockbuster, BATTLEFIELD EARTH, the biggest science fiction novel ever written. The unprecedented popularity of this saga led to it becoming a bestseller in countries around the world. In the U.S. alone it stayed on national bestseller lists for 32 weeks.

His final science fiction magnum opus was yet to come. After completing BATTLEFIELD EARTH, Ron sat down and did what few writers have dared contemplate—let alone achieve. He wrote the ten-volume science fiction (satire), MISSION EARTH. This fast-paced and humorous adventure, filled with biting social commentary on contemporary civilization, added a whole new dimension to the genre of science fiction. Once again, to the enjoyment of his millions of readers, L. Ron Hubbard had set a new trend.

But for Ron, that wasn't enough. He had spent a lifetime not only entertaining readers, but helping people. In 1984, he decided to give aspiring authors a hand in launching their own careers in the very competitive literary market. To that end, he began the international Writers of

The Future Contest, a short story competition for novice science fiction authors. The contest quickly expanded and yearly anthologies featuring the winning entries soon began appearing. This gained important recognition for the new authors who then went on to their own publishing careers. The prestige of this program grew, and in 1989, the Society Of Writers At The United Nations invited the annual L. Ron Hubbard Writers of The Future Awards Ceremony to be hosted at the U.N. itself. In that same year, another L. Ron Hubbard program was launched, this one to help new artists—The Illustrators of The Future Contest—and soon illustration entries from around the world began pouring in.

L. Ron Hubbard departed this life on January 24, 1986. His literary legacy includes more than 200 novels, novelettes, short stories and theatrical works spanning a wide variety of subjects including Adventure, Western Detective, Fantasy and Science Fiction. By the end of the 1980's, more than 44,000,000 of his fiction books had been sold.

Fiction books by L. Ron Hubbard are available in 66 countries around the world and have been translated into a dozen different languages. Unpublished works from his literary archives and the huge library of his existing classics will be made available, for years to come, as they are released for the first time in new editions and adapted for motion picture or television broadcast.

We, the publishers, are very proud to have presented to you one of L. Ron Hubbard's classic masterworks— FEAR.

ABOUT THE ILLUSTRATOR

Derek Hegsted lives in Provo, Utah. He earned recognition and prominence by winning the 1989 L. Ron Hubbard Gold Award for artistic achievement in the worldwide "Illustrators of The Future" Contest. Mr. Hegsted is currently doing illustration for major publishers of science fiction and fantasy.